The Tramp

SELECTED FICTION WORKS BY L. RON HUBBARD

FANTASY

The Case of the Friendly Corpse

Death's Deputy

Fear

The Ghoul

The Indigestible Triton

Slaves of Sleep & The Masters of Sleep

Typewriter in the Sky

The Ultimate Adventure

SCIENCE FICTION

Battlefield Earth

The Conquest of Space

The End Is Not Yet

Final Blackout

The Kilkenny Cats

The Kingslayer

The Mission Earth Dekalogy*

Ole Doc Methuselah

To the Stars

ADVENTURE

The Hell Job series

WESTERN

Buckskin Brigades

Empty Saddles

Guns of Mark Jardine

Hot Lead Payoff

A full list of L. Ron Hubbard's
novellas and short stories is provided at the back.

*Dekalogy—a group of ten volumes

L. RON
HUBBARD

The Tramp

GALAXY
PRESS

Published by
Galaxy Press, LLC
7051 Hollywood Boulevard, Suite 200
Hollywood, CA 90028

Printed in the United States of America.

ISBN-10 1-59212-332-5
ISBN-13 978-1-59212-332-2

Library of Congress Control Number: 2007903531

Contents

Stories from Pulp Fiction's Golden Age

A ND it *was* a golden age.
The 1930s and 1940s were a vibrant, seminal time for a gigantic audience of eager readers, probably the largest per capita audience of readers in American history. The magazine racks were chock-full of publications with ragged trims, garish cover art, cheap brown pulp paper, low cover prices—and the most excitement you could hold in your hands.

"Pulp" magazines, named for their rough-cut, pulpwood paper, were a vehicle for more amazing tales than Scheherazade could have told in a million and one nights. Set apart from higher-class "slick" magazines, printed on fancy glossy paper with quality artwork and superior production values, the pulps were for the "rest of us," adventure story after adventure story for people who liked to *read*. Pulp fiction authors were no-holds-barred entertainers—real storytellers. They were more interested in a thrilling plot twist, a horrific villain or a white-knuckle adventure than they were in lavish prose or convoluted metaphors.

The sheer volume of tales released during this wondrous golden age remains unmatched in any other period of literary history—hundreds of thousands of published stories in over nine hundred different magazines. Some titles lasted only an issue or two; many magazines succumbed to paper shortages during World War II, while others endured for decades yet. Pulp fiction remains as a treasure trove of stories you can read, stories you can love, stories you can remember. The stories were driven by plot and character, with grand heroes, terrible villains, beautiful damsels (often in distress), diabolical plots, amazing places, breathless romances. The readers wanted to be taken beyond the mundane, to live adventures far removed from their ordinary lives—and the pulps rarely failed to deliver.

In that regard, pulp fiction stands in the tradition of all memorable literature. For as history has shown, good stories are much more than fancy prose. William Shakespeare, Charles Dickens, Jules Verne, Alexandre Dumas—many of the greatest literary figures wrote their fiction for the readers, not simply literary colleagues and academic admirers. And writers for pulp magazines were no exception. These publications reached an audience that dwarfed the circulations of today's short story magazines. Issues of the pulps were scooped up and read by over thirty million avid readers each month.

Because pulp fiction writers were often paid no more than a cent a word, they had to become prolific or starve. They also had to write aggressively. As Richard Kyle, publisher and editor of *Argosy*, the first and most long-lived of the pulps, so pointedly explained: "The pulp magazine writers, the best of them, worked for markets that did not write for critics or attempt to satisfy timid advertisers. Not having to answer to anyone other than their readers, they wrote about human beings on the edges of the unknown, in those new lands the future would explore. They wrote for what we would become, not for what we had already been."

Some of the more lasting names that graced the pulps include H. P. Lovecraft, Edgar Rice Burroughs, Robert E. Howard, Max Brand, Louis L'Amour, Elmore Leonard, Dashiell Hammett, Raymond Chandler, Erle Stanley Gardner, John D. MacDonald, Ray Bradbury, Isaac Asimov, Robert Heinlein—and, of course, L. Ron Hubbard.

In a word, he was among the most prolific and popular writers of the era. He was also the most enduring—hence this series—and certainly among the most legendary. It all began only months after he first tried his hand at fiction, with L. Ron Hubbard tales appearing in *Thrilling Adventures, Argosy, Five-Novels Monthly, Detective Fiction Weekly, Top-Notch, Texas Ranger, War Birds, Western Stories,* even *Romantic Range.* He could write on any subject, in any genre, from jungle explorers to deep-sea divers, from G-men and gangsters, cowboys and flying aces to mountain climbers, hard-boiled detectives and spies. But he really began to shine when he turned his talent to science fiction and fantasy of which he authored nearly fifty novels or novelettes to forever change the shape of those genres.

Following in the tradition of such famed authors as Herman Melville, Mark Twain, Jack London and Ernest Hemingway, Ron Hubbard actually lived adventures that his own characters would have admired—as an ethnologist among primitive tribes, as prospector and engineer in hostile climes, as a captain of vessels on four oceans. He even wrote a series of articles for *Argosy,* called "Hell Job," in which he lived and told of the most dangerous professions a man could put his hand to.

Finally, and just for good measure, he was also an accomplished photographer, artist, filmmaker, musician and educator. But he was first and foremost a *writer,* and that's the L. Ron Hubbard we come to know through the pages of this volume.

This library of Stories from the Golden Age presents the best of L. Ron Hubbard's fiction from the heyday of storytelling, the Golden Age of the pulp magazines. In these eighty volumes, readers are treated to a full banquet of 153 stories, a kaleidoscope of tales representing every imaginable genre: science fiction, fantasy, western, mystery, thriller, horror, even romance—action of all kinds and in all places.

Because the pulps themselves were printed on such inexpensive paper with high acid content, issues were not meant to endure. As the years go by, the original issues of every pulp from *Argosy* through *Zeppelin Stories* continue crumbling into brittle, brown dust. This library preserves the L. Ron Hubbard tales from that era, presented with a distinctive look that brings back the nostalgic flavor of those times.

L. Ron Hubbard's Stories from the Golden Age has something for every taste, every reader. These tales will return you to a time when fiction was good clean entertainment and the most fun a kid could have on a rainy afternoon or the best thing an adult could enjoy after a long day at work.

Pick up a volume, and remember what reading is supposed to be all about. Remember curling up with a *great story*.

—Kevin J. Anderson

KEVIN J. ANDERSON *is the author of more than ninety critically acclaimed works of speculative fiction, including The Saga of Seven Suns, the continuation of the Dune Chronicles with Brian Herbert, and his* New York Times *bestselling novelization of L. Ron Hubbard's* Ai! Pedrito!

The Tramp

Chapter One

DOUGHFACE JACK unwedged himself from the rods with a startled grunt. He hadn't looked for the fast freight to stop in a Podunk like this and the thought of bulls had no more than flashed through his mind when he saw some legs coming and stopping at intervals along the cars. From the stick he knew it was an irate brakie, already twice dodged en route.

Anxiously Doughface sought to scramble out from under and so make the other side of the train. But the engineer backed a few feet with a jolt and, not knowing if it would happen again, Doughface took his chance.

He rocketed like a rabbit to the cinders and got one awe-inspiring glimpse of the six-foot brakie. He started to run, but in the other direction came somebody with a sheriff's paunch.

There was only one thing for it. The hounds had sighted the hare and Doughface couldn't trust his short legs on the level. He grabbed the handholds and started up the car.

"Come back here!" bellowed the brakie.

"Stop!" roared the sheriff.

Doughface scrambled for altitude as heavy boots ground cinders just under him. He was panting as he made the top of the car. He glanced back to see that the brakie was coming up the same way and the sheriff had taken the other ladder. The sheriff had a gun in his hand.

Doughface took a sweeping look at the town he had uncovered. An old gent waited at the crossing in a Model T Ford. A sign said "Centerville, Population 2,000." It was better than nothing. Doughface leaped for the other side and started down.

He would have been safe enough if his loose shoe sole had not jammed in the first rung. But jam it did and on that fact was to hang a national event.

He was still in sight on top and he yanked at the caught shoe. He heard a grunt and looked wildly about to see that the sheriff had made it.

"Stop!" bawled the sheriff.

Doughface almost had his shoe free. He gave one last yank and to the sheriff it appeared that the quarry was about to flee. He fired an intimidating shot—but the effect was more brutal. The bullet took Doughface in the shoulder. It slammed him out into space. His shoe held for an instant, long enough to turn him upside down.

He went through space like a bomb. He saw the switch he would hit and tried to fend for his head.

And then the lights went out.

Simultaneously sheriff and brakie appeared at the top to stare down.

The sight below was not pleasant and the sheriff gulped, "I . . . I didn't mean to hit him."

"Hell, he had it coming," said the brakie. "I got my orders. He was probably one of that gang of sneak thieves."

"Yes," said the sheriff doubtfully, "but . . . but maybe he wasn't, too."

The old man in the car had stopped his shaking machine. He reached hastily into the back seat and brought out a black bag and then, white hair streaming out from under his black slouch hat, he ran swiftly to the tramp. He gave one glance at the two on top of the car and the sheriff became red of face and nervously started to climb down.

The old man pulled Doughface away from the train and lifted his head for an inspection of the skull. The mass was as soft as a swamp.

The sheriff got down in confusion. "Hell, Doctor Pellman, I didn't mean to hit him. I was just . . ."

"First time you ever hit anything in your life," said Pellman. "Take his feet and put him in my car, Joe."

The sheriff was like a schoolboy caught with an ink bottle and a girl's braid. He gingerly picked up the tramp's feet and together he and Doctor Pellman succeeded in placing the man in the Model T.

"Get in and hold him from bumping," ordered Pellman.

Joe Bankhead cared more about the doctor's goodwill than he did about the bloody mess. He obeyed.

Pellman started the Model T and swung it around. He pulled the hand throttle all the way down and the rickety old car went galloping through Centerville to pull to a shivering halt before the doctor's office. The store loafers got up and peered interestedly.

"Been an accident?" they asked.

Joe turned red when he caught the doctor's eye and then

got very busy unloading the tramp. Together they packed him in and laid him on the doctor's chipped enamel operating table.

Miss Finch, the nurse, looked wonderingly at Pellman. "But he hasn't got any skull left, Doctor."

Pellman was already shedding his coat and rolling up his sleeves. He jerked his shaggy white head toward the door. "Get out, Joe. I won't have any time to hold your hand."

Joe shuffled out and closed the door behind him. Inside he heard Pellman saying, "Get that silver ice container Doris gave me for Christmas. I knew I could find some use for it."

Puzzled and downtrodden, Joe went back to the crowd on the walk.

"What happened?" they demanded.

Joe looked more uncomfortable than ever. "Aw, I couldn't help it. I got a wire to watch out for a gang that escaped from Cincinnati on a freight and I thought maybe this guy was one of 'em. But he was all alone and I guess he wasn't. I didn't mean to hit him." He was almost angry now. "He's just a damned tramp, anyhow!"

"Aw, you know the doc," said Durance, the storekeeper, wiping his hands on his apron. "Tramp or sick dog, he takes them all in. I tell him it don't pay. I've carried his accounts—"

"You wouldn't be here if it wasn't for the doc!" challenged Joe, pulling harshly at his gray mustache.

"Tha's so," said Blinks, the town drunk. "Ol' Doc Pellman'd own this town if savin' lives meant somethin'."

"All I said," defended the storekeeper, "was that he was too softhearted about his bills. I don't say he ain't a good doctor. . . ."

"An' you better not say it!" growled Joe, anxious to turn attention away from himself. "There's them that claim he's had fifty-leven offers to go to New York and be a brain surgeon. But he thinks too much of us, that's what. If he owed two hundred dollars to every store in town, it's still not enough to pay him back for what he's done."

"Think he can do anything for that tramp?" queried another loafer. "Fellah was pretty nigh dead from what I seen. Head all bashed in."

"Doc Pellman can do anything he sets his mind to," stated Joe.

They tuned their ears to the inside of the office and stood around almost in silence. They were awed by the thought that Doc Pellman might yank this tramp back from death, even though they had witnessed other things they thought miracles. Two or three times Pellman himself had gotten ill and that was the closest to panic that Centerville had ever gotten. They could not conceive a time when Doc Pellman wouldn't be walking down the street in his black coat and slouch hat handing out cheery hellos and free medical advice in every block.

Almost an hour later, Pellman came out. He was rolling down his sleeves as he looked at Joe.

"Will he live?" said Joe.

Pellman's big face relaxed into a smile. "If I could tell things like that, Joe, you could stop calling me 'Doc' and start calling me 'God.' How do I know if he'll live? That's up to Him."

"What'd y'do?" said Joe interestedly.

The doc's blue eyes twinkled. "Took off the top of his skull. There wasn't much left of it."

"Huh?" said Joe. "But . . . but what's he goin' to do for the top of his head?"

"I made a silver cap for him," said Pellman. "Out of that ice dish Doris gave me for Christmas. Knew it'd come in handy some time."

"Aw," said Joe, "you're foolin'. How could a man wear an ice dish for a skull?"

"Same shape and size," said Pellman. "If he's alive day after tomorrow he'll be as good as ever. Had to sew the two halves of his brain together but that hadn't ought to upset him. C'mon, Joe. I think you owe me a drink."

Chapter Two

DOUGHFACE woke up.

By some process of reasoning he could not define, he knew he had been in this cot for a week or more, but beyond that he could not go. Vaguely he remembered climbing up the side of a freight with a sheriff and brakie on his heels, but all was blank thereafter.

He moved his head a little and saw that he was in a small ward. It was not a regular hospital the way he had known them. It was apparently the back of a building and there were only three cots there. On the right-hand cot lay a man, dull-eyed and staring at the ceiling. On the left side was a young girl, face hidden by bandages and arm in a cast.

Doughface Jack lifted himself up on his elbow. The springs creaked loudly and that must have been what Miss Finch heard. She came in from the office beyond and saw that it was the tramp.

Doughface blinked confusedly. This girl wasn't bad looking—blonde and slight—but she had a mole on her chin. Doughface thought it didn't look good there.

"Hello," she said cheerfully. "How do you feel?"

Doughface looked cautiously around him. This wasn't a jail hospital and he took courage. "Aw, I guess I'm okay, sister."

"For a man that's been through what happened to you, I'd

say you looked marvelous," smiled Miss Finch. That was not exactly true. Doughface had always been as fat as a butterball and his complexion had never been anything but pasty white. The bluish growth of beard did not help.

"What's the idea?" said Doughface, glancing around again.

"You mean where are you?" said Miss Finch. "Doctor Pellman saw you get hurt and brought you here. He operated."

"Geez," said Doughface, alarmed, "I ain't got no lucre. Them things cost the bucks!"

"Never mind," said Miss Finch. "The doctor hasn't collected a bill for years and he doesn't even try anymore. You can thank him for your life."

"Huh," said Doughface, "he must be a right guy."

"He's a wonderful fellow, if that's what you mean," said Miss Finch.

"Y'mean I'd be dead if it wasn't fer him, huh?"

"That's it."

"Geez . . . And he don't want no lucre for it?"

"No," replied Miss Finch. "Now you be quiet and I'll go get you something to eat."

"Eat?"

"Yes. Anything you want in particular?"

Doughface shut his eyes and then gathered courage to take the plunge. "How about chicken and ice cream?"

"All right," said Miss Finch.

Doughface blinked. He suspected this wasn't Earth after all. If it wasn't for that mole this girl would look just like . . . Huh! He gaped at her in astonishment.

"What's the matter?" said Miss Finch.

"That . . . uh . . . y'had a mole on yer chin and it ain't there no more!"

Her hand flew to the spot. She stepped to a mirror at the head of the bed and stared at herself. "Why . . . why, that's so. It's gone!"

Through it all the man on one side had not moved and neither had the girl practically hidden in bandages.

Doughface did not long concentrate on the vanishing mole. "What burg is this?"

"Centerville," said Miss Finch in a preoccupied fashion, hand to chin.

"Then this is all the hospital there is, huh?"

"Yes."

"What's the matter with these ginks?" said Doughface nodding his head to right and left.

"That's Tom Johnson," said Miss Finch. "He's dying of cancer and the doctor is going to operate later in the day. And this is Jenny Stevens. She was in an accident last night—poor thing. You had better be very quiet. They're very sick."

"Jake with me," said Doughface. "You mean it about that chicken and ice cream?"

Miss Finch smiled and went out.

Doughface turned over and regarded the man for some time. The fellow was barely conscious and at long last he turned his head.

"How ya feel, pal?" said Doughface.

The man's lips moved but no sound came forth.

"Hard lines," said Doughface sympathetically.

The man moved his lips again and this time he spoke.

11

"Heart's almost gone. But I hope Doc Pellman's gonna fix it. I know I wasn't none too good but . . ."

"He saved my life," said Doughface. "I guess he's a right guy."

"Shore is," said the man, strongly. "He brung my four children into the world. Ain't nobody hereabouts that'll say nothin' agin Doc Pellman."

He stirred restlessly and looked long at Doughface. Slowly he raised himself up on an elbow and further regarded the tramp.

Unexpectedly Tom Johnson said, "You got a cigarette, cap'n?"

"Me? Naw. They was some snipes in me clothes but I don't see nothin' around now."

Johnson raised himself higher and glanced around the room. An ashtray was under the window and he could see the butts in it. He swung down his feet and stretched. He shuffled across the floor and fished out a butt. He found some matches and brought the tray back to Doughface.

Again Johnson stretched and then took a luxurious puff. "Ain't enough air in here," he said, crossing to the window and throwing it open. He stood in the chill blast, again stretching.

"My goodness but I feels good," said Johnson.

Doughface was disappointed a little, but grinning just the same. "Yeah, I put on an act like that plenty of times. What'd you want, some free meals?"

"Ac'?" blinked Johnson. "Say, Doc Pellman was wrong. He said I was gonna die maybe. But I ain't gonna die. I feels like I could lift this buildin' sky-high."

Doughface grinned knowingly. The girl in the other cot stirred a bit and Doughface turned to grin at her. "Whatcha know about that, sister? Tom here pullin' a fake to squeeze a free handout from a right guy like this Pellman."

The girl turned her head painfully to look at Doughface. Her voice was very faint. "What?"

"I said Tom was tryin' to gyp the old man. But what the deuce. I done it myself lots of times. What was you doin'? Neckin' party or one arm drivin' or somethin'?"

The girl stirred. "Drivin'?" Until that moment she had not realized where she was. She started to put her arm down and found that it was in a cast. The weight of bandages on her face was suddenly smothering to her and she pried them away from her mouth and nose.

"How long have I been here?" she queried.

"The nurse said since last night," said Doughface. "She claimed you was on a wild party. . . ."

The girl sat up straight. "I was not! The other man was at fault. He was on the wrong side of the road! Was Bob hurt?"

"Who's Bob?" said Doughface.

The girl looked wildly around her to make sure Bob wasn't there.

Miss Finch came in at that moment with a tray for Doughface—chicken, ice cream and all. She saw Johnson standing by the window in his nightshirt and gave a gasp of horror.

"Get in bed!" cried Miss Finch. "You're due to be operated on in an hour!" She turned and saw the girl sitting up. "For heaven's sake! Lie down! You've got a compound fracture and your face . . . Jenny Stevens! What have you been doing to your bandages?"

The girl pulled at the gauze so that she could see better and Miss Finch stopped dead.

The nurse managed to recover her wits. She advanced on Jenny and moved the gauze again.

"But it can't be!" cried the nurse. "That eye was out! There was an inch splinter of glass in it! But . . . but maybe it was the other eye." She lifted the other bandage and a healthy blue orb blinked at her in a puzzled way. "I must have been mistaken. . . ." said Miss Finch shakily. "But . . . but no. I wasn't! I held your eye open while he took the glass out. He said you couldn't ever see again."

"Where's Bob?" pleaded Jenny, not too interested in Miss Finch's observations.

"Why . . . why, he's been outside all morning. He broke his nose and his arm but we let him go home."

"Bring him in," pleaded Jenny.

With misgivings the nurse brought Bob to the door. He was limping and his arm was in a sling and his face was almost hidden by adhesive tape.

"Jenny!" cried the boy. "Then you'll live! I . . ."

"Sure she'll live," said Doughface unexpectedly. "No dame sits up in bed and looks at a guy that way if she's on her way out." With a tramp's boldness he added, "You goin' to marry her?"

Bob stared at Doughface. "Why . . . why, I guess so."

"Y'ain't bad lookin'," said Doughface.

"Do you mean you would?" said Jenny to the boy.

"Why . . . gee . . . I been tryin' for months to get up nerve . . ."

She held out her arms to him and he freed his own from the sling and held her close.

"PLEASE!" cried Miss Finch. "Bob Tully, you'll compound that fracture if you don't stop that nonsense!"

"Fracture?" blinked Bob, staring at his arm and moving it around. "Why . . . why, it feels perfectly all right." He stepped back. "But it's stuffy in here." He pulled at the adhesive tape on his face.

"STOP!" cried the distrait Miss Finch.

It was too late. The tape was off and other than the marks the stuff had made, there was nothing else wrong with Bob Tully's face.

Miss Finch tottered to the window and shoved Tom Johnson aside. She leaned out into the air and finally got herself composed. When she turned around the girl was stripping the cast from her arm and with dull eyes Miss Finch watched her. She was not even shocked when she saw that there was nothing wrong with that arm.

"What's the matter with you?" said Doughface. "You shouldn't get mad just because everybody's been goldbrickin' on the doc. Hell, I done it lots of times." He sat up straight in bed. "Cheer up."

Miss Finch instantly smiled. Suddenly she could not repress an impulse to approach Doughface. She picked up the tray and put it before him and then she kissed the bandaged top of his head.

"Whatcha doin'?" gaped Doughface.

She too was confused about it. "Eat your chicken."

"May I have my clothes?" said Jenny Stevens.

Tom Johnson saw that he was in a nightgown and quickly slid back into his own bed. "Mine too, Miss Finch."

"Aw, what do you want with clothes?" demanded Bob Tully. He threw a blanket around the girl and picked her up in his arms.

"Where are you going?" demanded Miss Finch.

"Why . . . to carry her home," said the boy.

"But that's half a mile!"

Bob juggled her weight in his arms and frowned. "Why, you don't weigh much more than twenty pounds. That's funny. Maybe you're lighter or I'm stronger."

"Please," whimpered Miss Finch. "I don't care what you do but get out before I go crazy."

Doc Pellman was in the doorway. "What's all the noise back here?" he said, smiling. And then the full import of what he saw struck him. A dying girl was beaming into the face of a boy who carried her with a fractured arm. And a man dying of cancer was smoking a cigarette and giving him a white-toothed grin. And there was something changed about Miss Finch too. She was prettier than before.

"Doctor," said Miss Finch. "I don't . . ." and there she stopped in amazement, staring at Pellman.

Doughface, at the sound of "doctor," had looked up from his chicken with great interest to beam upon his benefactor. All eyes were on Pellman now.

An old man had stood in that doorway. His shoulders had

16

been stooped and his white hair shaggy and his face seamed with kindly wrinkles.

Pellman had not moved, did not seem aware of any change in him.

But now his hair was curly and brown and his face was that of a man of twenty-one. His shoulders were square and almost bursting through his black coat. His long-fingered hands were not wrinkled now. Only his eyes were the same and they were still kindly and wise.

Bob Tully dropped his girl back to the cot in astonishment. Tom Johnson's eyes were like teacups. Miss Finch was open-mouthed and if she had not seen the doctor's graduation picture—class of '96—upon the wall of the office, she would not have known this fellow at all.

He was still Doctor Pellman.

But he looked four years younger than he had on the day of his graduation from medical college. His staid, elderly clothes struck Miss Finch as ridiculous now and she began to laugh, almost hysterically.

"What's the matter here?" said Pellman, concerned with what he had seen and now worried about Miss Finch. He strode forward and faced around again. "Has everybody gone crazy?" He stared at Miss Finch. "My dear girl, what on earth is so very amusing?"

"You!" choked Miss Finch. "You look like you stole those clothes from a scarecrow."

"My clothes?" said Pellman, taken aback.

"Your clothes," said Miss Finch.

Pellman took himself to the mirror to see what had happened

17

to his suit. But he forgot that instantly. He stared at his own image. Suddenly he snatched the mirror from its hook and gazed at it in amazement, turning it over after the fashion of a child expecting to see the other child. He looked again and winked an eye to be sure it wasn't an old photo of himself. He opened his mouth and made a face. So did the mirror.

In consternation he whirled around, again looking at his nurse and patients. Tom Johnson was nearest and Pellman slammed him back on the cot and began to tap the region around his heart. More amazed than ever he advanced on Bob Tully and pushed at the perfectly normal nose. He whipped the boy's sleeve up and examined the arm to find no sign of abrasion or break. He picked up Jenny Stevens' arm and studied that, finding it a normal arm when it should have been a compound fracture. He pushed her back and poked his fingers around, unable to again discover the broken ribs which had pierced her lungs. Finally he hauled the bandages from the face which had been unrecognizable for its cuts and breaks. Jenny Stevens was more beautiful than ever.

Pellman whirled on Miss Finch. "What happened in here? What . . . Say! There's no mole on your chin!"

Again she touched the spot and again was bewildered.

"Can this be me?" said Pellman, picking up the mirror. "Can this be we?"

"'Smatter, Doc?" said Doughface, gnawing a chicken leg. "I was thinkin' you was an old geezer. Thought you was for a minute. But that ain't nothin'. I sure want to tell you that I think it was pretty swell, you fixin' me up. Whatja have to do t'me?"

Pellman looked steadily at the grinning tramp. The man had not appreciably changed and was still not wholly well. Pellman examined the edges of the wound and then saw that the scalp which covered the silver skull had healed very rapidly.

But alone in all that room, Doughface Jack was the only man not perfectly cured.

"Want some more chicken?" said Pellman irrelevantly.

Chapter Three

DOCTOR PELLMAN, the following day, paced up and down the middle of his office in deep thought. He had some medical books open on his desk, pages flopped out as though they had expired.

Miss Finch sat by the window looking down into the street. Every time she glanced at the doctor she received a distinct shock. It was disconcerting to work for two years with an elderly, fatherly gentleman and then suddenly have him turn into an athletic youth who might have posed for a collar advertisement. It was also disconcerting to have this young man keep calling her "child" and "young lady." And it was also very hard to remember to address him with due respect.

Pellman stopped and with a savage sweep sent the medical books thudding to the floor. "Damn it! I tell you there's no answer that I can find. Cancer does not cure itself in an instant! An eye will not heal of itself so swiftly. A broken arm is a broken arm and compound fractures are compound fractures!"

"And moles are moles," said Miss Finch.

"Yes! Moles are moles! And they don't just vanish like that unless something is done to them. I tell you, young woman, I laid awake all of last night trying to get an answer and I'm still hunting!"

Miss Finch looked at him and thought he was more handsome than ever when he became so wild in his gestures and so dynamic in his excitement. Nobody in her memory had ever seen Doctor Pellman that excited.

He stomped over to a mirror above the washbowl and stared at himself. He ran his hand over his smooth jaw to make certain it was real. He faced her anew.

"And as for me, I'm either crazy or . . . Say, maybe I'm crazy. Look," he said, striking a pose, "am I or am I not a . . . an aged patriarch?"

"You look like a college boy," said Miss Finch, heart thumping. "You . . . you're very handsome."

"That's it. I . . . What did you say?"

"I said you were very handsome."

Pellman crossed to the mirror again and looked at himself. He let down a little and smiled. "Sure. I used to be quite a boy. Say, Miss Finch, I think I'll get some clothes. This frock coat doesn't look so good on me now, does it?"

She smiled and shook her head.

He examined his face again. "Huh. If I don't watch myself some young lady is going to set her cap for me."

"Yes," said Miss Finch quietly, involuntarily touching her white cap.

"And I'm talking like a fool, too," decided Pellman, all business again. He resumed his pacing up and down the floor, shaking his head as he went.

At the end of a long time he came to a decisive halt.

"Miss Finch, I may be wrong. It may be the tramp and it might not be the tramp. I've got to make a test."

She got up expectantly.

"Miss Finch," said Pellman, "you go down the street and find Sarah Bates and her consumption. Find a kid with warts. Nice, big warts. Find old 'Thunder' McClain and his grouch. Locate Mrs. Toby's youngster, the one with eczema. And bring them here. Bring anybody here with a cold or a headache. Go get 'em!"

Miss Finch slipped into her jacket and went swiftly out. Pellman walked back to his ward and entered.

Doughface Jack was lying in bed, propped up with pillows and admiring a view of a peach tree outside the window. He heard the door open and turned to beam at Pellman.

"Geez, Doc, this is the nuts. I been sick a few times in my life, but I'm tellin' you, I never thought it could be like this. I feel tops, I'm tellin' you. I'd get up if . . ."

"You stay where you are," said Pellman, moving to his side and pulling out a cigar case. "You're perfectly well today and you ought to be sick as a dog for another month at least. Have a smoke?"

"Y'mean I hadn't ought to be well?" said Doughface Jack, taking two.

"By all the rules and regulations as hereinbefore stated, you shouldn't have lived in the first place. But you did and here you are and you're perfectly all right."

"Y'mean," said Doughface, looking sad and wistful on the instant, "that you're goin' to boot me out of here, Doc?"

"Listen, fellah, quit that panhandling snivel and light up."

Doughface grinned instantly. "Y'know y'way around, dontcha, Doc."

23

"A man that's handled all the sickness of Centerville for forty years ought to," said Pellman.

Doughface blinked. "Forty years? Hell, y'stringin' me. You won't be forty for another twenty years."

Pellman was about to contest the point with severity when he suddenly remembered. He shrugged and touched his lighter to the tramp's cigar.

Doughface sat back, drawing his knees up, folding his arms and puffing contentedly. "Chicken and ice cream and now a ten-cent cigar. Yeah, Doc, this is the nuts. Anythin' y'want done, now, just say the word. I'd even chop some wood for you."

"You've got something to do," said Pellman. "Listen, a lot of my friends are coming up here to pay you a visit and you be on your good behavior, understand?"

"What do they want?" said Doughface, suspiciously. "I been up against Ladies' Aid Societies before this, Doc, and I ain't . . ."

"No, nothing like that. You just lie there and say nothing. I'll do all the talking."

"You're the boss," said Doughface, puffing away.

Footsteps sounded in the outer office and then Miss Finch was at the door, gazing in admiration for a moment at Pellman.

"Yes?" said Pellman.

"I brought them," said Miss Finch, recovering herself with a start.

"Show them in," said Pellman. "No . . . wait. I'll talk to them first."

He went into his office and there were his guinea pigs in

various stages of disorder. Sarah Bates was feeling very poorly and wanted everyone to know about it, gazing sadly with blue eyes too large for her sallow, thin face. A small boy was very suspicious of the proceedings and had his hands behind his back because Miss Finch had spotted the warts on them. He was very ashamed of his warts.

Thunder McClain was stumping about, muttering to himself, bent over and twisted with arthritis and meanness and old age. Mrs. Toby's youngster was backed into a corner, conscious of eczema and wondering what was going to happen. Storekeeper Durance sneezed loudly and blew his nose on his apron.

"Good people," said Pellman, "I . . ."

"Won't!" said Thunder McClain defiantly. "See here, Doc Pellman, you order . . ." He stopped, his watery eyes growing wide. He had not seen Pellman for three days. "Huh? Who are you? I thought I heerd Pellman talkin'."

"I am Pellman," said the doctor.

"Hogwash!" stated McClain. "Y'think I wouldn't know Doc Pellman if I seen him? Maybe you think I'm blind too! See here, you young whippersnapper, nobody is goin' to order me around unless I knows what's happenin'!!"

"Good people," said Pellman, again. "I . . ."

"Doctor," whined Sarah Bates, "I think I am going to faint."

"Postpone it for a moment, Miss Bates," said Pellman. "I called you here to show you the result of an interesting experiment in surgery."

"Humph," said McClain.

"As you are among the best citizens of Centerville," said Pellman, "I wanted to show you something very unusual. Now, if you will please follow me I'll be greatly obliged."

They followed without much interest. Pellman led them into a half circle about Doughface Jack's bed and they came to a halt and fidgeted.

Doughface Jack removed the cigar from his mouth and looked to Pellman for his cue.

"Jack," said Pellman, "I want you to meet these very good friends of mine. They are much interested in your case." He saw Doughface start to don his panhandling expression and checked him. "The town has already taken up a collection for you."

Doughface grinned and stuck the cigar back in his face.

"This is Sarah Bates," said Pellman.

Doughface grinned at her and nodded and then went on smoking.

Sarah Bates raised her nose at the odor. "Doctor, it is a little close in here and I am feeling . . ." She tried to cough but could not make it.

"Miss Finch!" said Pellman. "Wait in the outer office, Miss Bates."

The elderly woman tried again to cough and was greatly perplexed at her inability to get more than a clear sound. Doughface thought it was funny and his grin broadened.

"And this," said Pellman, hurriedly, "is Mr. McClain."

"Humph," grumbled Thunder McClain. "Never thought I'd have to be introduced . . ."

"Of course not," said Pellman swiftly. "But Doughface is going to be a pretty famous fellow, Thunder."

Doughface beamed.

"Miss Finch!" said Pellman.

"This is Durance," said Pellman. "He wants to know if you want some cookies."

"What?" said Durance.

"He's got a whole store full," said Pellman.

Doughface beamed again.

"And Jimmy here," said Pellman, "wants to shake hands with you, Doughface. He's a real tramp, Jimmy."

The small boy advanced cautiously and held out his hand. Doughface took it, felt the roughness of it and looked at it. "Huh. Warts. Y'know how to cure them things, kid? Y'take some punk-water at midnight in a graveyard and say real fast, 'Devil, take my warts!' and zing! they'll go just like that!"

Doughface snapped his fingers and the boy stared at his own hands. "Why . . . why, gee whiz, Doctor Pellman. Gee whiz, I . . . why, what happened to these warts?"

"And this is Jullie," said Pellman quickly.

Doughface beamed on Jullie, Mrs. Toby's child.

"Now get out, all of you," said Pellman, shooing them off.

He went back into his office. A young man in baggy corduroy was there fumbling with a crooked cane and looking in perplexity at a young and beautiful woman who, from time to time, tried unsuccessfully to cough.

"Look here," said Thunder McClain to Pellman, "you ain't goin' to fool me none, young feller. When I see Pellman and tell him you been makin' free with his office and patients, he'll give you suthin' to think about. An' what've you done with Miss Bates?"

The lovely blonde looked up in surprise. "Why . . . why, you sound just like Thunder McClain." She peered at him carefully. "But no! That can't be! Thunder McClain wouldn't get married when he had a chance and he's never had a son . . . and yet . . . yet you look just like a son would look if . . ."

"I AM McClain," stormed the youth, banging his cane down.

"Doctor," begged Miss Bates, "are you going to let a poor maiden lady be bullied by this young fool?"

"Young fool?" cried McClain. "Young woman, I'll have you know . . ."

"Stop it," said Pellman, pulling the mirror off the wall and handing it to McClain. "Look at yourself."

McClain looked grudgingly and then suddenly gaped at his image. He looked at Pellman but he couldn't get a word out.

Pellman took the mirror away and shoved it at Miss Bates. She gazed at it without interest at first and then she, too, suddenly realized that something had changed.

She felt her fresh skin. She opened her mouth and looked at her tongue. She held the mirror back and saw the rounded curves which had taken the place of her flatness.

"Why . . . why . . ."

"Yes," said Pellman, "it's happened. You are now possessed of the wisdom of fifty and the youth of twenty. Both of you. And a long time ago, I seem to remember, you were both twenty with no more sense than to quarrel over some trivial thing. You have your chance again."

They were stunned.

"Get out," said Pellman.

They edged toward the door, looking at each other. Thunder McClain loosened his collar, "Gosh, Sarah, you look just like you did that there night when . . ."

"Don't," said Sarah Bates pleadingly. "Let's forget, Thunder. For thirty years I have known that I was wrong. . . ."

"*I* was wrong!" cried Thunder McClain.

"Oh, Thunder," said Sarah, "you're . . . you're just like you used to be and . . . and I love it."

Pellman heard them going down the steps and then remembered that the two children and Durance were still there.

"Let's see your tongue," said Pellman to Durance. "Ah . . . just as I thought, young fellow. Your cold is gone."

"Why . . . why, so it is," said Durance, remembering. "Gosh, did I get young too?"

"I'm afraid you did," said Pellman. He handed the mirror to Durance.

He took the two children by the shoulders and led them to the window. Jimmy he examined for warts and found none. Jullie's eczema had vanished. He gave them a quarter and pushed them out of his office.

Miss Finch sat down at the window in a daze. "It's happened again. It *is* the tramp that does it."

"Yes. But why? That's what I want to know. WHY?"

Pellman resumed his pacing up and down the floor. Miss Finch sighed.

"Wasn't it beautiful?" said Miss Finch.

"What?" demanded Pellman.

29

"For thirty years they have lived apart and alone and now they can come together at last. . . ."

Her final sigh was so gusty that he stared at her. For a moment she thought he understood as a light came into his eyes.

But she was wrong.

"I've got it!" said Pellman excitedly. "I'll get hold of Professor Beardsley in New York. He's been monkeying around with such things. He'll know!"

He grabbed for his telephone and Miss Finch, disgusted, listened to him start the call.

Chapter Four

M OST excitement this town's had in years," said Sheriff
Joe Bankhead, pulling at his mustache. He sank down
in a chair across from Pellman and signaled for some beer.
Then he dragged out a bandanna and mopped at his face.
"That shore was a crowd, Doc. Thought we'd never get the
way clear for them to get aboard."

Pellman poured his glass full. But he did not drink. His
young face was pensive and he was staring thoughtfully into
the great distances.

"How come all this happened?" said Joe. "I can't git it
through my thick skull that you're you. I seen you yesterday
and almost before I thought I almost said, 'Hello, sonny.'"

Pellman smiled. "Can't say as I'm used to it either, Joe."

Joe noisily drank his beer and then wiped his mustache.
"Was them real honest-to-God professors and things, Doc?"

"Real honest-to-God professors, Joe."

"I still can't figure it out. What would professors want with
a tramp?"

"I hope they know," said Pellman. "I was sorry to . . . Oh,
well. What the devil. After all, I didn't have a bill of sale on
Doughface Jack."

"I kinda figure he didn't like leavin' you, Doc. He kept

lookin' at you after he got on the platform like he was minded to stay."

"Joe, it isn't right. I have a feeling it isn't. Something may happen."

"What? He ain't dangerous. He's just a tramp."

"Just a tramp," echoed Pellman thoughtfully.

"Well, ain't he?"

"Joe," said Pellman, "that 'tramp' could do more for this world than any other living man. With a glance he can cure anything. But . . ."

"Yeah, I heard somebody say that. But I think it's the bunk, don't you, Doc? How could a thing like that happen?"

"You saw what happened to those people that went in to see him all last week," said Pellman.

"Yeah, but . . ." Joe shook his head. "How could a thing like that work, huh?"

Pellman smiled wickedly. "Have you ever heard of mito-genetic rays, Joe?"

"Huh?"

"Mito-genetic rays. They were first discovered as coming from onions. 'Mito' means 'a thread' and 'genetic' is the same as 'generator.' 'Thread-generators,' then. Onions grow better when there are a lot of onions around. But no weeds grow in an onion patch. Onions, throwing out mito-genetic rays, kill weeds and benefit other onions."

"Huh? How come?"

Pellman shrugged.

"What's that got to do with Doughface Jack?" said Joe.

"I put his brain together. I had to sew up the two halves because of skull splinters and such. That's the first time I know of that the two halves of a man's brain have been connected. And then the entire brain is under silver, which will carry most currents. That's as close as I can get."

"Y'mean Doughface Jack has an onion in . . ."

"No," said Pellman. "Every man has those mito-genetic rays in his head and nerves. Almost any human can look at yeasts and kill them just by looking. For instance, you could kill the yeasts in that beer just by staring at the beer and concentrating. . . ."

"Huh?"

"Anyhow," said Pellman, "by connecting up his brain and short-circuiting the wave action I didn't hurt his thinking process but I increased his generation of mito-genetic rays. Consequently, when he looks in kindly fashion at another person he can cure that other person of anything."

"Yeah, but . . ."

"Look," said Pellman. "When you come into a room you can tell the man with the most magnetic personality there. Some people make you feel good and others make you feel bad. That is a slight reaction of mito-genetic rays. But onions can cure each other, evidently, by that process and kill out weeds."

"Huh," said Joe, slumping down. "Gimme another bottle of beer. Doc, all I can see is Doughface Jack walkin' around with an onion instead of a head."

"Another beer here," said Pellman. He stared thoughtfully

at it as he poured it and then sipped at it without much enthusiasm.

"Y'worried?" said Joe.

"A little," said Doc Pellman. "The world isn't full of onions, you know."

Chapter Five

DOUGHFACE JACK was highly elated. He had just done a very clever thing. He had walked out of the university and clear down to Central Park without once being molested. He chuckled about it, very pleased. Although he enjoyed being lionized in the clinics and though the newspaper stories and the pictures of him tickled his fancy, he had been in New York for two months—and being two months in one place was akin to agony to the wanderlust of the tramp.

And so he strolled in the sunshine, easy despite the stiffness of his clothes. Birds were caroling and he could almost imagine that he was in a jungle. Of course, all these people on the walk were not exactly to his taste and the cars which went by on the drive made a lot of noise. But still, even this small freedom was preferable to being dogged night and day by men with thick glasses.

And all would have been well, even then, if a debutante had not fancied herself very powerful in the control of two white wolfhounds.

She came posingly along the walk, dogs straining at the leashes with well-bred eagerness, and glancing around to see if anybody noticed. The girl was wholly unaware of a putty-faced little fellow who came toward her and he was oblivious of her.

At the moment he was watching the clouds roll high overhead. And so he bumped squarely into the wolfhounds and trod on their tender toes.

Instantly they snarled and snapped.

Doughface Jack leaped back, unmanned for the moment. He had a tramp's true distrust for dogs and he saw two raging beasts, so it seemed, charging to devour him.

He saw he could not run. He must meet them as they sprang.

He mustered up his fighting courage and the two wolfhounds fell dead.

It was as simple as that. One minute they had been springing and the next they lay like two doormats of wool upon the walk.

The girl stared at them in disbelief and then at Doughface Jack. Abruptly she whirled. Far away she spotted a mounted policeman coming on the trot to see what all the snarling had been about.

"HELP! POLICE!" screamed the girl.

"Please," begged Doughface. "Please, ma'am. I didn't do nothin'!"

She turned again, glaring and shaking with hot rage. "You murderer! I saw you knife them!"

Doughface Jack blinked at her and then he got just a little bit mad himself.

The girl's anger faded. She put her hand to her face and her knees became wobbly.

Instantly Doughface was concerned.

The girl stood up straight, mad all over again and very blistering in her language.

He saw he could not run. He must meet them as they sprang.
He mustered up his fighting courage and the
two wolfhounds fell dead.

"What's goin' on here?" snapped the officer. He started to get down from his horse.

Doughface saw danger. Too many years he had run from cops not to run again. In panic he took to his heels. But fate was not kind. There was no way through the hedge along the walk.

The officer heard the girl's first few words and then he vaulted back into the saddle. With spur he sent his mount rocketing after the fleeing tramp.

Doughface saw that he was done. He envisioned a striking club and perhaps another hospital. He saw himself losing all his prestige. The Law was on his trail.

He could run no farther.

He turned around. He saw he could not win but he had to do something. He struck a belligerent pose.

And the policeman's horse dropped dead with a mighty crash, spilling the officer to the concrete.

He was not hurt and even as he rolled, the policeman fought to blow his whistle. He blew it, springing up. He glanced at his dead horse and then grabbed Doughface Jack by the arm.

The tramp was shaking with terror. He had not one ounce of scrap in him now that the Law had him securely.

"Please," he whimpered. "I didn't mean nothin'. I was just out walkin'. . . ."

"Mister," said the tattered officer, "you got some questions to answer. That was Miss DuVrois back there and . . . and the guy that kills my horse is goin' to sweat. Plenty!"

And other cops came running at last and Doughface Jack,

shaking as though with the ague, certain of his doom, afraid to show any fight, was wheeled off to the precinct to the tune of a wailing siren.

Doughface Jack was caught in an avalanche of blue which bore him out of the wagon, up the steps of the station house, down dingy corridors and into a room where sat a desk sergeant of large dimensions.

"Book this guy for disorderly conduct," said the outraged mounted patrolman, "until I can sweat some real crimes out of him!"

Again the wave picked up Doughface Jack and hurled him along a corridor and into a room where a white light glared. Doughface landed in the chair and the light bored into his skull and faces ringed him 'round.

"Please," he whimpered. "I didn't mean ta . . ."

"Howja kill them dogs?"

"Howja kill my horse?"

"C'mon, talk!"

"Ja use a knife?"

"Whereja throw it?"

"Y'know this might mean a year in the pen?"

"Howja kill them dogs?"

"Please!" moaned Doughface. "I didn't do nothin'. I'm the guy with tha-tha eyes. C-Call up tha university. C-C-Call Professor Beardsley. I . . ."

"So ya won't talk!"

"Howja kill them dogs?"

"PLEASE! I'm the guy with tha EYES! Call Professor B-B-Beardsley. I didn' do nothin'. I . . ."

"So ya won't talk!"

"Howja kill my horse?"

"PLEASE!" wailed Doughface. "I don't know. Things happen and I don't know! I tell you, y'gotta call Professor B-B-Beardsley."

One of them heard him and grabbed a phone and the third degree was about to begin when he came back.

"Wait! Beardsley said this was the guy with the mito-something eyes. Y'know. In the papers."

"Yeah, but my horse . . ."

"Please, please, please," moaned Doughface. "I . . ."

"Wait!" cried the man who had phoned. "This guy's got somethin' screwy about him. He can cure anythin' he looks at." He had their attention now. "And Beardsley says for God's sake don't make him mad!"

Doughface couldn't see very well because of the light but he could sense the way they suddenly drew back. He could see the awe. He sat up straight and scowled, testing it out. They drew back further.

Doughface understood now. They were scared of him or at least they weren't going to jump him. He had to put up a front and get out quick before they jailed him.

He kicked at the lamp and it spun, taking its light from his face. The officers bristled anew.

Doughface got halfway out of his chair. He was glaring now, getting mad and acting dangerous in the hope that he could cow them.

And an awful thing happened. The men began to get wobbly. One grabbed hold of the table for support and then his knees buckled, letting him down. Another backed to the wall and slipped from there to the carpet. The mounted officer fell flat on his face.

In Doughface Jack's brain rang the words of Pellman, "Don't glare at anybody, Jack. Something might happen." It was happening all right. And he was glad of it.

The last man collapsed before him. They were not dead. He could see them breathing with difficulty. But he had learned something, had Doughface. He had killed dogs with a glare. He had killed a horse by a glare. He had knocked these men out though he was still scared of them.

He marched to the door. He felt too big to walk in a corridor, and though his size had not increased, his perception had.

Abruptly he realized what would happen to him if he was found here with these knocked out cops and in a panic he rushed out into the corridor.

The desk sergeant saw him coming and recognized nothing but an escaping prisoner. He surged up and leaped to block the tramp's way, brandishing a nightstick.

Doughface started to say, "Please," but the sergeant was coming too fast. There was no retreat. Doughface took a deep breath and squared off for a glare.

The desk sergeant did a complete somersault and landed at Doughface Jack's feet. He was breathing but he was a mighty sick man.

Further panic hit Doughface. He dashed like a frightened rabbit out into the street.

41

Chapter Six

L IKE the little boy passing the cemetery, Doughface Jack tried to appear casual and still keep alert. But for all that he had to walk rapidly. He was sick at his stomach from the portent of doom which overhung him. Regardless of its mito-genetic powers, his brain was a maelstrom of confusion.

It was far beyond him to understand what had happened. He could only draw conclusions insofar as his experience would allow. He knew definitely that cops carried clubs and hit people over the head.

He had no great terror of jails. He had seen too many when booked for vagrancy. He had sometimes worked himself into jail when the nights were cold. But he knew that cops carried clubs and brakies carried clubs and in that lay his entire horror.

More than once his scalp had been bruised and bloodied by a nightstick and the resulting headaches had filled weeks with misery. And now he had another thing bothering him.

Pellman—and he still thought he could trust Pellman—had told him that he would have to be careful of a fall. "You get a dent in that tin skull you've got, Jack, and it's liable to be the end of you."

Of course the skull wasn't tin. Tin that thick would have had some resistance. But tin rusted and so the skull was soft, pliable silver. One blow from a nightstick and he would be a dead man. Doughface Jack knew that. He had no faith in anything after a man's lights went out and he was very anxious to stay on an earth which had been pleasant to him. One blow on the head and he was done.

Cops were such unreasonable people, he thought as he scurried along uptown. Could he help it if a couple dogs dropped dead and if a horse collapsed? Was it his fault? Did he do it on purpose?

No!

And had he asked those cops to bully him that way? And had he deliberately knocked them for a loop? And, therefore, was it his fault if they fell on their faces?

No!

But cops, he thought, were dumb. They couldn't understand those things and the next one . . .

And there he was, standing on the corner swinging his nightstick and watching the parade of baby carriages go along the park walk.

Doughface Jack's heart was a chunk of alum. He slowed down. He sauntered. He eyed the trees and sky and attempted to whistle. The officer had not yet heard the broadcast and though he thought that this pasty-faced little fat man was acting suspiciously, there wasn't any real reason to accost him.

And so, for the instant, Doughface Jack got by.

Fifty feet ahead was a crossing and the lights were against Doughface. He was much too interested in the bluecoat behind him to see the truck coming. It was an enormous thing grumbling under the weight of great rolls of sheet iron. The driver was a New York truck driver. He had the weight and he had the right of way and so he stuck his broken nose in the air and sailed serenely along and let the pedestrians fall where they might.

Doughface heard the rumble when he was almost under the wheels of the juggernaut.

With a yelp of fright, the tramp skipped back.

"Watch where ya goin'," snarled the truck driver in passing.

And then an awful thing happened. The driver collapsed over his wheel and the truck careened toward the curb. Pedestrians screamed as they scurried back. Over the curb went the truck, over the curb and over the sidewalk and straight into a plate-glass window the size of a billboard.

There was a splintering crash, the rending of metal and the sudden shriek of the patrolman's whistle down the block.

Doughface Jack waited to see no more. He started to run and banged squarely into an officer coming from the other direction. He bounced off at an angle and that officer, thinking it was suspicious, tried to grab Doughface. Abruptly he was flat on the walk.

"Hey you!" bellowed the other one behind Doughface.

The tramp spun about. He wasn't risking being either shot or struck from behind. He knew what he could do now. He glared and the patrolman banged to concrete with a grunt which faded out into a moan.

When Doughface took wing this time he barely touched pavement for blocks. He dashed over crossings and through crowds driven by terror and the necessity of finding refuge at the university.

He beat the mile record getting there, vowing with each

sturdy puff that he would never again walk these streets if he got out of this scrape alive. If possible he would leave New York and return to the rods. Starvation was preferable to such danger.

So blind was he with sweat and exhaustion that he almost leaped up the steps of Professor Beardsley's house without examining the ground. But sunlight hit on a brass button in the nick of time. Doughface dived for the shrubbery and peered carefully forth.

The front steps were an entire bank of blue cloth. Fortunately all the officers had been facing the door and they had missed him. They were not entering, it seemed, but waiting for their superiors to come out.

It was a chilling sight.

Doughface, panting as silently as he could, thought fast. He could not stay on the streets. His name had been plastered all over New York and his picture had appeared so often that he could never hope to escape exposure. He felt naked without strong walls around him.

He withdrew cautiously and hurried down the block. He turned the corner and then headed into an alley. He knew the back of Beardsley's house because he had often had the pleasure of talking to the garbage man there. And so, with great stealth he tiptoed up the steps and eased into the kitchen. The officers would not search the house. They wouldn't think he was here. And besides, Beardsley would help him out of this jam. Beardsley would tell them the truth.

He started to enter a hall when he heard voices in the study.

He got down and put his eye to the keyhole and found that he was looking at Beardsley in profile at his desk.

"Gentlemen," said Beardsley, "I tell you once more that he is not here. You can search the house if you like."

"Maybe he'll come back," muttered a police captain.

"We'll wait," decided an inspector.

"Gentlemen," said Beardsley, tears in his voice, "believe me when I tell you that I had no slightest inkling of his potentialities."

"Yeah," said the police captain.

"But believe me!" said Beardsley, polishing his pince-nez in agitation. "I took pity on him, a poor, helpless tramp. . . ."

"You made yourself famous with him," stated the inspector.

"Gentlemen, in the interests of humanity, science will even condone vulgar publicity."

"Y'didn't tell the newsmen that," said the captain. "See here, Professor, your university . . ."

"My university," said Beardsley, "has no responsibility in the matter whatever and neither have I. There is in existence no contract establishing any connection for responsibility between the university and myself and this tramp. What he has done is regrettable, true. But to expect the university to act as guardian angel to a tramp—a mere tramp, gentlemen—that is going too far."

"Y'mean you'll turn him over to us?" said the inspector hopefully.

"He has broken the law," stated the professor, growing bolder. "And for that he must suffer."

"If them guys die," growled the captain, "it's the chair for him."

"Justice must be served," said Beardsley in a devout manner.

"Say, look," said the captain, "how come you didn't suspect that this hobo could kill things by just lookin' at 'em?"

Beardsley took refuge in scientific lore. "Mito-genetic rays are almost wholly unknown. No great amount of work has been done upon them. We were experimenting. That was all. Evidently as long as this tramp is in a jolly frame of mind the rays are beneficial to the recipient. But when this man's anger is aroused, then the rays become so intense that they not only kill all foreign bacteria and stimulate cells and tissue but they destroy those cells themselves. By destruction of such cells, a man is instantly made to suffer from acute anemia. And there is a telepathic factor which seems to enter. Generating fear, this tramp makes another man feel afraid at long last. Generating rage, he makes other men rage. Generating cheer, he makes others cheerful. Emotional telepathy, the commonest kind. . . ."

"I didn't come here to listen to no lecture," growled the captain. "All I want is to get my grub hooks on that hobo. We'll show him a thing or two."

"Perhaps," said Beardsley, "if you make a cordon about any part of the city where his presence is known you can sneak up on him. I must warn you that if he is given a chance, no amount of police can cope with him."

"You mind if we . . . ah . . . find it necessary to shoot your guinea pig?" said the inspector.

48

"It would be a loss to science," said Beardsley. "But—the man is dangerous. We have no claim or hold upon him, no responsibility to him. . . ."

"Even though he got you a five-million-dollar donation," said the disgusted captain. "C'mon, Inspector. The circles of the mighty make me sick to my stomach. Let's go out and nail that tramp."

"Professor," said the inspector, "if he comes here, you will, of course, quietly call us?"

Beardsley pondered. It was dangerous to be in line with Doughface Jack now. "Inspector, I can probably find a way to put some heavy sleeping powder in his food."

"Good," said the inspector.

"Huh," said the captain in disgust.

Doughface watched Beardsley's eyes follow them to the door. Inside, the tramp was shaking like jelly. He saw Beardsley get up and approach the door and he scurried back into the kitchen and out into the alley.

"Them guys," said Doughface as he went over the back fence, "is just a bunch of stuffed shirts after all. They're y'pals until y'get in trouble—Pellman and all the rest of 'em!"

Chapter Seven

SHERIFF Joe Bankhead raced, for all his bulk, into the office of Doctor Pellman. His mustaches were waving in the wind he made and so did the paper in his hand.

"DOC! I just got . . ." he puffed for a moment. "I just got a long-distance telephone call from THE CHIEF OF POLICE OF NEW YORK CITY!"

"Well," said Pellman, leaning back in his swivel chair. "So you're gettin' famous, eh, Joe?"

"No. Listen. Y'know that Doughface that left here three months ago?"

"I ought to," smiled Pellman.

"Now look, Doc, you got to go to New York or somethin'. It's awful."

"New York. Why? Miss Finch and I were thinking of getting married tomorrow—or hadn't you heard by some strange coincidence?"

"Yeah, sure. But listen, Doc, that Doughface has gone crazy. He killed some cops and a truck driver and . . ."

"Whoa," said Pellman. "Take it easy."

"Well," said Joe, taking a long breath, "the Chief of Police of New York told me that Doughface Jack got loose and the first thing he done was murder a desk sergeant. And then a flock of cops trailed him and tried to take him and he killed all of them. And then a detective tried to pot-shoot him from a window but Doughface seen the gun and looked up and the detective fell out the window, stone dead. And then Doughface walked into a restaurant—the Waldorf, I think it was—and when they wouldn't serve him without some clothes on—I dunno if he's goin' naked or not—why, the headwaiter fell down dead and so did another guy behind him. And then this Doughface walked out and the hotel dick drew his gun and Doughface killed him. The whole town's on its ear, Doc. Nobody knows what to do. Doughface Jack is walkin' around and killin' people just by lookin' at them and the place is in an uproar! The chief remembered the case and he called me to see if I could make you grab a plane or train and get the hell to New York and stop this Doughface. But . . . but . . . Gosh, I never thought of that!"

"What?" said Pellman.

"Why, he'd probably kill you too!"

Pellman got up and lighted a cigarette. Musingly he looked into the sunlit street. "Poor fellow," he said feelingly.

"Poor feller, be damned!" said Joe. "He's killin' guys right and left. First thing you know, he'll get the idea of robbin' banks and then maybe he'll decide to run the country. And nobody can stand up to him. The governor ordered out the National Guard with machine guns but they won't arrive until tonight!"

"WHAT?"

"The governor . . ."

"I heard you! Miss Finch!"

She came swiftly.

"Pack a grip. Anything, you understand! Call the Cincinnati airport and tell them to send a ship, any ship, over here to land in that pasture south of town. I've got to get to New York. They're going to kill Doughface."

"But," said the sheriff, "they'll *have* to kill him! He's . . ."

"I did that to him. I'm responsible. Quick, Miss Finch."

Chapter Eight

DOUGHFACE tried to obliterate himself by merging with the crowd which poured into the subway at five. He hid his face and did the best he could to keep from being recognized, but it wasn't any use.

A man was coming up the steps with a newspaper in his hand and the front page of that tabloid was given up wholly to Doughface Jack's visage. The man glanced up as he bumped into somebody and stared straight into the tramp's face.

The man turned white and a strangled shout left him, "IT'S THE MAN WITH THE EYE!"

A second later the only person on the subway steps was Doughface Jack. He sighed deeply and pushed his hat back from his round, pasty face. He picked up the paper which had betrayed him and read the sad story.

EVIL EYE STILL LOOSE
TRAMP TERRIFIES CITY

Doughface Jack, until lately renowned as the panacea for all human ills, is still at large after three devastating days.

One murder and countless cases of assault have already been committed and police fear more.

Washington expressed the grave concern that the man might acquire delusions of power and seek to dictate governmental policies. . . .

Doughface threw the paper down in disgust. "Geez, them guys is dumb!"

He stepped back to the street, abandoning any idea of hiding in the subway. But an astonishing thing had occurred.

Here he was at Broadway and Forty-second Street and not a single human being was in sight. He saw an office window slam but that was all.

Miserably he plodded along. This was very different from his late affluence. Not one man could he talk with. Everybody knew his face by this time. Nobody would run the risk of being sent to the hospital. Even auto traffic would careen out of his way. That truck driver that had almost run him down had plowed through the Macy's display window when Doughface had happened to glare.

If those cops would only leave him alone!

The one thing he did not feel bad about was the detective that had tried to pot-shoot him. Seeing that gun had almost killed Doughface with fright, but he had remembered to glare just in time. Of course the detective had fallen, but that was his hard luck.

Two or three times he had paused before jewelry store windows and now he paused again. He heard a door slam in the back of the shop and looked curiously inside. The dealer in diamonds had been putting away his trays and they still lay upon the counter. Doughface picked up a few and then let them trickle back. Of what use were diamonds? He couldn't find anybody to spend them on and no dame would dare face him long enough to be offered one.

He plodded out of the store and back to the street. His appearance caused two men who had ventured forth to dart inside a building. Doughface looked glumly toward the spot.

No, they didn't want to end up in the hospital. The newspapers said that all patients would recover but that one glance from Doughface would land a man in a hospital bed for two weeks.

He turned up deserted Seventh Avenue. He was very thirsty and he eyed the signs as he passed. Far behind him traffic was cautiously beginning to move once more.

Doughface stepped into a beer parlor and saw with relief that nobody there had heard the street commotion. He was almost to Fifty-fifth Street and maybe that accounted for it. The bartender came up with a professional smile. "What'll ya have, buddy?"

Doughface felt like a dog feels when he wags his tail. "Gimme a beer," said Doughface.

The bartender reached for a glass and the tap. But just then a man in a booth stood halfway up, a newspaper gripped in his fist, his eyes round as dinner plates as he stared at Doughface.

"It's him!" screeched the traitor. "It's him! The man with the Evil Eye!"

Chairs crashed and glasses splintered and feet thundered. And then everybody was gone except Doughface Jack and the man who had called him by name. The traitor lay in the sawdust, unconscious and pale.

"It's him!" screeched the traitor. "It's him!
The man with the Evil Eye!"

Doughface quietly tasted his beer but his melancholy was so deep that he could not enjoy it. He put a dime on the counter and wandered back to the walk. Again the news had spread and cars were stalled and abandoned in the street. Nothing in sight moved, though an El roared like surf in the far distance.

"Geez," sighed Doughface, "I ain't got a friend in the world. What wouldn' I give to be in a jungle cookin' up some rotten meat in a tin can!"

Shoulders hunched, he plodded northward and into Central Park.

The lights were just coming on and the day was sadly faded and it is this period when it is the most difficult to see, having neither sun nor complete night. Pedestrians had lost sight of Doughface Jack. They had not expected him to walk this deeply into the park.

And it was with relief that he found himself trudging with a crowd again, his hat pulled down over his face and his eyes upon the ground. There was something very soothing in this mingling with humanity once more as it is very hard to be a pariah. Doughface was enjoying this association to the limit. He grinned a little to himself as he went and bit by bit he had begun to regain some of his spirit. He straightened up gradually and was finally walking fully erect.

Darker and darker it became and, by contrast, the more penetration did the park lights possess. Higher and higher rose the brim of his hat from his face.

He could not stand prosperity.

He was swaggering along at last and a man with half an eye could have recognized him—and so it was not so strange that a man with two eyes did.

He was walking around a fountain and the light was very bright. There were many people here, out for an evening stroll. A beggar woman was selling pencils on a bench, sightless eyes cast down behind her black glasses. She was trying to look humble.

Doughface passed her without a glance the first time and marched straight into the glare of the park lights.

A man and woman were coming toward him in the crowd and the man was paying more attention to the woman than he was to his right-of-way. He bumped into Doughface and glanced up with a scowl.

The pasty complexion could not be missed; the round face and the peculiar glow in the eyes which, in this light were almost as luminous as a cat's.

The man staggered as the recognition struck home. He opened his mouth to yell and strove to pull the woman away. Doughface knew what was coming. He tried to shout a warning himself and beat that warning scream. But all he did was glare.

"IT'S HIM! IT'S THE MAN WITH THE EVIL EYE!"

The man said no more. He collapsed on the gravel. There was a surge of the crowd and Doughface Jack was left in a swiftly widening circle. The woman was kneeling by the man, striving to pull him to his feet.

Doughface felt bad about it to see her braving death to get her man to safety. She was a worn looking woman. . . .

But suddenly she was stronger and just as suddenly her man got dizzily to his knees and, with her help, limped hurriedly away with fearful backward glances.

"Geez," said Doughface, standing all alone. "It's happened again. Damn the luck anyhow!"

There was no use going deeper into the park. The police might be around and he had better change his location with speed.

The beggar woman had been knocked from the bench in the rush. Her pencils were scattered in the gravel and a few dimes and nickels were lost beyond her blindness.

And Doughface was running. The old beggar was just getting up, her hands snatching at the pencils like claws. Doughface was not looking for anyone to be down on their knees. He kicked her solidly and fell over her. The jolt made lightning flash behind his eyes, stunning him for an instant.

She had screamed with pain and now she sat rocking back and forth in agony, clutching at her side. One hand went out to support her and she touched Doughface Jack's shoe.

She knew he was still there. She caught her breath sharply and then, for all his years in the jungles, Doughface Jack felt the impact of real cursing which carried hate behind it with every foul gasp.

She called him everything a sergeant could think of; she tore his ancestry apart, blasted his possible progeny, accused him of all the diseases known, attacked his personal habits and withered him with sheer obscenity. And all in a shrill, awful whine which was blasphemy itself.

Doughface Jack was stunned. He did not know what he

was doing. He heard the words, saw the source and anger flashed like powder burning in his eyes.

And she crumpled. She sank down like an empty sack dropped in the dirt. One hand was outstretched, fingers barely touching a pencil and the other still clutched her side. Her breathing was slow and laborious and loud; it took no second glance to see that in an instant she would be dead.

Doughface Jack sat up straighter. His brain was clearing and he understood what he had done. He looked at her.

The coat was colorless, dirty and torn. Half a neckpiece was clumsily sewed to it with burlap thread. One stocking was twisted and lumpy about her leg and the other was a man's. Her shoes were all the way through and her dirty soles were bare. The hat was a pitiful attempt at jocularity with its bumptious feather still waving. Her skin was so tight across her bones that it seemed no skin at all but parchment.

Her face was little more than a skull with cheekbones like brassy doorknobs. Her nose was swollen with drink. And her glasses had fallen away to disclose those awful sightless eyes now staring inwardly at the gathering blackness of death. They were no more than holes in her face, those eyes, with great sooty shadows spreading out from them across the seamed flesh.

She was horrible.

But Doughface Jack saw the pencils and he saw the torn sign, "I am Blind." Doughface Jack knew what it was to be cold and hungry and alone.

He hitched himself forward to her across the gravel. He glanced around to see if any police were coming. He tightened as he thought he caught a siren's far-off moan.

He came closer and touched her shoulder. "Please," he whimpered, misty-eyed. "Please, I didn't mean it. I got knocked out too and I didn't know what was the matter. Gee, I wouldn't of killed you if I'd knowed. You GOT to believe that! I wouldn't 'a' hurt you."

He shook her roughly. "Look, don't kick off. Don't make me know I killed you. Gee, I been on my uppers myself, I know . . ." He sank back. "God, I wish I was dead. Nobody can look at me, nobody can be near me. . . ."

But she had stirred. She was struggling to rise a little, pain still gnawing at her skeleton face.

Doughface sat up too. With a surge of hope he leaned toward her. "Gee," he cried excitedly, "maybe you ain't gonna die! Gosh! Look, it's all right. If y'wanna, I'll go getcha a hamburger. I'll getcha a steak and . . . an . . . an . . ."

The impacts of the shocks hitting her were enough to make her shiver like a machine-gunned soldier. But she straightened more and more. She left off propping herself up.

"That's swell!" cried Doughface gleefully. "Look, I'll getcha anything you want. I can have anything I want. All I gotta do . . . Come on, thata girl!"

He jumped up and helped her to her feet and then he stooped to get her glasses and pencils. He handed them to her and she looked at them wonderingly.

"For God's sake," cried Doughface with great joy. "You can see!"

"Yes," she said dazedly. "I . . . I can see!"

Stupidly she gazed all around her. "Why . . . why, it's night and I thought it was still day."

"C'mon, I'll see you home," said Doughface, jumping like a puppy at the thought of being able to talk to somebody, anybody.

"And that . . . that's the fountain I've been hearing for years," she said wonderingly.

"Y'been blind that long?" said Doughface.

"Since I was twenty-three. I'm sixty-one now." She laughed a little shakily. "Something must be terribly wrong—or right. Why is it that I can see?"

"It's me," said Doughface. "I used to do that all the time before . . . before a dumb cop got mad and chased me on his horse. And for days and days I been walkin' around and every time . . ."

"Oh," she said in sudden understanding. "I heard somebody say something about you. They said I ought to go see you but I thought it was just another one of those bunko schemes. They're all bunko schemes."

"I ain't," defended Doughface stoutly.

She glanced around her again and saw that a popcorn vendor had deserted his post. There was candy there and popcorn and she was starved. Swiftly she moved toward the cart and into the bright light of the park lamps beside the splashing fountain. With eager hands she snatched up the bags and then, with another sly glance about her, she emptied the till into her pocket.

"Hey," said Doughface, catching up with her. "Nix on that put-together, sister. Stealin' ain't goin' to go. I'd get blamed for it."

"And why not?" she said defiantly, whirling on him.

He caught his breath and stopped dead.

Suspiciously she stared at him. "Well, what's the matter now? I know I ain't no lily to look at."

"No-N-No!" stuttered Doughface protestingly. "No—geez—it ain't that. It's . . ."

She had changed. How radically she had changed!

Her eyes were black and fiery like those of a Spanish dancer. Her face was a perfect oval and the skin was fresh and delicate of color. Her teeth were white and flashing and her hair was glossy and ebon. Her hands were smooth and each nail upon them was perfect.

She followed his gaze to her hands and looked at them herself. She gave a start. "Why . . . why, I thought they were . . . rough!"

Doughface Jack didn't know just why but he couldn't swallow. He could feel the blood throbbing in his veins and he was lightheaded and wanted to shout but there was still something worshipful about the way he felt.

She was the loveliest thing he had ever seen anywhere. She was a wondrous, vibrant girl as soft and pliant as silk and yet there was steel in her too. He was awed.

She took a quick step to the fountain and looked down at her reflection. She glanced at Doughface Jack.

And her voice was hushed.

"You did this to me. I heard but . . . but I didn't believe. And now, now I'm as I was the day the fire made me blind!"

"Gee," whispered Doughface, "you're swell!"

In a sudden ferocity of distaste she looked at her rags of clothes. She ripped at the coat with offended hands and cast it from her.

She looked like a girl of seventeen, as sweet and innocent as a beautiful woman could be at that age.

But one thing had not changed. Behind those flashing eyes was a mind packed with the lust and chicanery of thirty-eight years of begging and sixty-one years of life.

She knew. She stopped ripping at her clothes and stared at Doughface Jack. "I've heard lots about you," she stated slowly. "I've heard them talking here in the park and on the streets. They're afraid of you. The police can't stop you. All you have to do is look at a man and that man can no longer stand. Yes, Jack, I have heard a great deal."

He was too happy to be near her to care too much what she said. He was glowing with companionship.

"Yeah," he said disinterestedly.

"They've tried to shoot you and club you but they can't. All you have to do is look upon them and they drop. . . . Jack."

"Yeah?"

"Listen, Jack, has it occurred to you that you could have anything you want in the whole world?"

"Yeah, but what's the use . . . ?"

"Use?" she cried with an exultant laugh. "Use? Why, you precious fool, can't you *see* it?"

"What?" said Doughface.

Her voice was sibilant and lovely. "It would be easy," she said, "for you to rule the world."

He wasn't paying much attention in that instant. A rumble

was in the air and whistles shrilled from afar. He stepped swiftly to a crosswalk and stared at the street a block away. An Army camion was there and men were leaping out of it, rifles with bayonets fixed gleaming in the light. A machine-gun crew was hurriedly slamming their weapon on its tripod.

"Geez," said Doughface, terrified, "we got to get out of here! It's the Army!"

Chapter Nine

DOUGHFACE JACK was thoroughly frightened. He snatched at the girl's arm and strove to head her around the fountain and across the park. She, too, was infected by his terror and followed blindly.

He brought up short. He had seen bright buttons gleaming across the park and he heard a camion roaring there as it surged to the curb to discharge its men in olive drab.

Doughface took a dozen false steps north and again he heard camions. He whirled in a panic and again skirted the fountain striving to get out of the trap to the south. But there was no exit there. A hundred men in company front were marching across the lawn straight toward them.

Doughface felt sick. He could feel a steel-shod rifle butt clanging down upon his silver skull. His mind, lacking any solution, was, for the moment, completely blank.

The girl shook herself as though she had been drugged and was just coming to life. She took check on the situation. Doughface Jack was patently too much in a funk to meet these soldiers, and the soldiers, just as clearly, were there to shoot Doughface on sight.

But they had only guessed that their quarry was here. Outposts had reported no man passing them. Doughface must then be somewhere within an area a block square and every inch of that area would be covered.

She could save herself. It would be easy to scream for help and thereby avert death by bullets. And life, at last, tasted very sweet to her.

But she didn't. She grabbed Doughface by the shoulder and yanked him into the shrubbery. Against his amazed face she slapped handfuls of dirt. She roughed up his clothes. She bashed in his hat. Then, on hands and knees, she went back to the bench where she had so lately sat and located the dark glasses, the tin cup, a few nickels and some pencils.

She put the glasses on Doughface.

"Whatcha doin'?" he complained, shivering as he listened to the marching feet which drew nearer and nearer.

She broke a stick from a shrub and pushed it into his hand. "Haven't you ever panhandled?"

"Yeah," said Doughface, "but I can't figure these so'diers would make such hot suckers."

"Be still and follow me."

She crawled back to the gravel, Doughface after her. Suddenly she shoved him to earth. "Don't move. Just moan!"

Doughface got it. He drew himself up in a knot and moaned piteously.

"HELP!" screamed the girl. "IT'S HIM! IT'S THE MAN WITH THE EVIL EYE!"

Doughface thought for an instant that he was betrayed but when he glanced up and saw the innocence of her beautiful face his doubts were vanquished.

"HELP!" screamed the girl. "There he goes! There he goes!

Ooooh, Father! Father, speak to me! Oooooh, he's dead. I know he's dead!"

Whistles shrilled in the darkness. Boots thudded over the lawns. A young lieutenant, his face white with strain, charged up, automatic in hand to behold a beautiful woman weeping.

"Ooooooh, I know he's dead," she moaned. "I know it! He killed him, he killed him!"

"Quick, lady, which way did he go?"

"Oh, he's dead, I know he's dead!"

Doughface pushed out a moan and drew up in a tighter knot. The "I am Blind" sign was still on the gravel. The tin cup and pencils and dark glasses told their story well as did the scattered coins which gleamed in the lamplight.

"Quick, damn it," said the jittery lieutenant, "which way did he go?"

"Oh, my father, my poor, poor father," moaned the girl.

"For GOD'S SAKE!" cried the lieutenant, "are you going to let that murderer get away? Which way did he go?"

The girl pointed with a trembling hand. "That way," she choked. "That way. The beast! To strike down a poor old blind beggar . . ."

"We'll get 'im!" yelped the lieutenant. His whistle shrilled and he signaled with his arm for his men to come up on the double.

The other sides of the square were closing in.

"He's over there in those shrubs!" cried the lieutenant.

"Clear the way beyond!" bellowed a captain.

"Machine guns!" roared a major. "Rake that shrubbery!"

71

Machine gunners began to trip their chattering guns. Bullets whipped and sang a deadly chorus through the shrubs.

"Company A," roared the major. "Into line!"

"Company advance!" cried the captain. "CHARGE!"

They charged the cover and bayonets flicked and stabbed through wood and earth.

"Nothin' here!" cried a sergeant.

"He's got to be there!" yelped the lieutenant. "That old man and girl . . ." He pointed and then stopped, looking foolish.

The old man and the girl were gone.

And they were running with all their might and the shrubs took long strips from their clothing. They were going south back toward Times Square.

"Y'all right?" panted Doughface.

"Never felt this good in my whole life," said the girl. "If we can get into the thick of it those soldiers won't dare shoot. Keep hold of that cup and those glasses!"

"I got 'em," puffed Doughface.

A sentry loomed before them. He saw them and started to raise his rifle and shout at the same time. The sentry went down in a heap.

The driver of a camion saw them coming a hundred feet away and he started to shout. But Doughface had seen him first. He slumped over his wheel, arms loose and dangling.

A taxi was cruising past. The girl was startled by it. She had not thought that a taxi looked this way.

And Doughface stopped it, careful not to knock the driver out. Doughface thrust the girl into the machine.

"Drive," said Doughface.

"Where?" said the startled cabbie.

"Fifth Avenue," stated the girl. "I've always wanted to see it."

The cabbie gave them a sour look. He could judge people very well by the kind of clothes they wore. "Y'got any money, pal?"

"Sure," said Doughface, reaching into his pocket.

But he didn't have any money.

"I thought so," said the cabbie. "Gwan, scram, y'dead beats!"

Doughface had no time to think about it. The cabbie went sideways into a pile under his meter. Doughface was aghast.

"Can you drive?" he asked the girl.

"Of course not. Can you?"

"I th-think so," said Doughface. He popped out and then into the driver's seat. He had seen it done often enough. He crashed the gears into reverse, saw that he was wrong and ground them brutally into high.

His luck held. The car started ahead and Doughface sat up straight and gripped the wheel hard enough to crush the wood.

The girl looked back anxiously. Some soldiers were coming and whether or not they would connect the cab with Doughface was a problem. But Doughface had his hands full already without further worry. The taxi was lurching like a bucking bronc.

They came to a crossing and the light was against them. Doughface was a little slow on finding the brake and through they went. He looked around hopelessly, thinking certain a policeman would see. But none did.

His luck was still holding.

He made it into Fifth Avenue, nursing the throttle to discover what happened where. "Geez," he called back, "this is the nuts."

"Don't go too fast," begged the girl. "This is the first time I was ever in a car."

"Don't worry none," said Doughface, exuberant in his control of power. "I'll . . ."

But he didn't. A yellow and green bus stopped squarely before him and he missed the brake with his foot. He had barely time to twist the wheel violently to the right. Belatedly he found the brake and tromped on it, coming to an abrupt stop almost up against a parked limousine.

He was bewildered. He knew he couldn't get out of this without making a scene and if he gathered a crowd that would be a tip-off to the soldiers twenty blocks behind.

For a moment he strove to back up and get out. But it was too much in his excited state.

"We gotta beat it," said Doughface, leaping out.

The girl was by his side as he raced to the walk. Already an inquiring officer was walking slowly over toward the curiously parked taxi.

Doughface had the glasses on again and the tin cup in his hand. The girl led him.

It gave her a sense of power she had never known to be finding the way for another human being. Always it had been herself that had been led. It was wonderful not to have to stop uncertainly to search for a curb, poking about with a stick, hoping that somebody would take pity. . . .

Chapter Ten

DOCTOR PELLMAN paced nervously across the carpet of the police commissioner's office. A National Guard colonel, New York's police chief, the commissioner and two inspectors sat and watched him.

Each time Pellman would stop, all the men would sit up straight and open their ears expectantly. But always Pellman resumed his pacing, more worried than before.

At last he stopped, tall with anger, before the colonel. "If you had only waited ten minutes," he said, shaking his finger under the colonel's nose, "we would now have all this straightened out!"

The colonel looked at his shiny boots and his face got cordovan. "I had my orders!"

"Yes, you had your orders," said Pellman, "but damn it, man, you also had my wire." He shook his head hopelessly. "If you'd only *thought*."

"Soldiers don't think," said the colonel gruffly. "They obey orders."

Pellman turned to the police commissioner and his young face was strained. "You're responsible for this too, remember," said Pellman. "If you hadn't let that broadcast order go out, Doughface Jack wouldn't be so much on the *qui vive*."

"The what?" blinked the commissioner, removing the long cigar from his orator's mouth.

"At every turn he expects to be nabbed," said Pellman. "He's scared to death. He's no killer. He's just a poor chap that was unlucky enough to be the object of a miracle. He probably didn't even know he could kill people just by looking at them until he met those thick-headed fools that grilled him."

"They paid for it," growled the commissioner.

"Sure, half of them are dead. But what they did is being paid for by others—good United States citizens. Don't forget that," stated Pellman.

"Sure," ventured an inspector, "they're payin' all right. About a third of these people he's looked at are dead by this time and the other two thirds are dying. I say he ought to go to the chair."

"*You* say it," said Pellman. "Then why the devil don't you go out and get him?"

The inspector squirmed. "I . . . er . . ."

"I know," said Pellman, striding up and down the rug again. "I'm responsible for this. It's up to me. I put his brain together and therefore I'm the killer. . . ."

"Ah, nuts!" said the commissioner. "You didn't have anything to do with it. How'd you know what was going to happen?"

Pellman paid no heed. He gave very little evidence of being what he was—a small-town doctor. He showed none of his decades of wisdom in that youthful face of his. But he had been room companion to death so often that people alive or dead could not impress him very much.

"Turn the militia on him!" growled Pellman to himself. "And now what will he do? He won't show his face in New York. He'll try to leave the city and head for the country and then we've pushed him beyond any chance of getting him at all. There'll be no tracing him just as soon as he gets beyond the radius where he has been publicized. And the stupid papers. Running his face on every front page of every edition. You'd think they'd be able to realize something once in a while. Of course when a man calls him by that silly name, Doughface gets mad and it begins all over again. But he can walk down an avenue through an entire crowd and, unless he's molested, nobody hears a thing about it."

"Professor Beardsley is still waiting," said a clerk through the inter-office phone.

"Let him wait!" barked Pellman savagely. "The stupid fool. He ought . . ."

"Sssh," said the commissioner. "That phone worked both ways."

"What if it did? Gentlemen, it's not often I get mad and I wouldn't be angry now if it weren't for that cowardly fool out there. I don't dare meet him. I'd kill him. All he had to do was to tell Doughface that everything was all right and Doughface would have allowed himself to be confined in some country estate with perfect happiness."

"Huh," said the colonel. "I'm not worried about Doughface Jack's happiness. He's done for two of my men, remember?"

"What if he has?" said Pellman. "Was it his fault?"

"His fault or not," said the commissioner, "he'll swing, I'm afraid. Murder, Doctor Pellman, is, after all, murder. And whether it is done with the eyes, a knife or a gun, it is still murder."

"And you'll use more force," said Pellman in disgust. "I . . ."

The phone jangled and the commissioner grabbed for it. The man at the other end was shouting so loudly that Pellman could hear it halfway across the room.

"I tella you, I'ma Grik. I'ma gooda Grik. But he come inna here, he knocka me down, he taka da clothes, he poota da rope ona me and thissa gal, she go widda heem. He feexa me right. He makka me so small I slide outa da rope."

"Did you hear where they were going?" demanded the commissioner.

"Sure. Why you think I call? They go to da train. They go to da Washington and taka da country. They ona way righta now. You gotta do asomething. Me gooda da Grik. I losa . . ."

The commissioner banged the phone on the hooks. "They're heading for the station. That'll be Pennsylvania. Come on!"

Chapter Eleven

TRYING to appear indifferent, Doughface Jack and Rita entered the Pennsylvania Station. They wore street clothes at Rita's express command, and they carried luggage which had been growing heavier and heavier block by block. Suntan powder helped mask Jack's identity. Redcaps assaulted them and wrested the bags away.

Doughface was upset. "How we gonna pay?" he whispered for the hundredth consecutive time.

"Never mind," said Rita with a mysterious smile.

He was not at ease in this expansive place. The ceiling was too high and the other walls too far away and the crowd which milled consisted of far too many. The uniformed redcaps and trainmen and guards gave him an uneasy chill. It was all right for Rita to be so cool about all this. She hadn't done anything and she wouldn't be shot on sight or burned later.

He sidled up to the ticket window, the fashionable black hat well down over his face. "Gimme," he said nervously, "two tickets to Washington, DC."

The clerk nodded and began to pull out green slips.

"Drawing room," whispered Rita.

"Huh? Oh—yeah—drawing room, mister."

The agent reached for his phone and checked for a reservation. There was one and he began to prepare the slips, from time to time looking expectantly at Doughface for the money.

Doughface felt a wad of bills thrust into his hand. He blinked at them and then shoved them through the wicket. After the tickets and change had been given back to him, he pulled Rita aside.

"Whereja get it?"

"Now, Jack, don't be cross."

"Whereja get it?" he repeated roughly.

But she smiled at him and he melted on the instant. "A man with a diamond stick pin had it in his pocket," said Rita winningly. "He didn't need all that money anyway and, besides, I put the wallet back."

"The wallet . . . why . . . Say, what . . . ?"

"You don't think a beggar, and a blind beggar at that, wouldn't learn to take advantage of New York crowds, do you?" challenged Rita.

Remembrance came as a shock to him. Here was a glamorous woman in expensive blue sports clothes—a woman who had so lately worn a sign which said, "I am Blind."

She didn't let him think about it. "Let's get aboard right away before something happens."

He followed her and the redcaps followed him and they hurried toward the gates.

Doughface Jack didn't recognize Pellman until the doctor stood squarely before him, seemingly from nowhere.

"Geez!" said Doughface, skidding to a halt. "It's . . . it's you, Doc."

"Yes, Jack, it's me. Listen, fellow, don't you think this has gone far enough?"

Doughface looked downcast. "Yeah. Yeah, but how can I stop it? The cops is all chasin' me and the Army come out tonight. Geez, Doc, them guys is goin' to shoot me on sight. That's what the papers say. This is a helluva put-together. I can't do nothin' but run."

Rita came back, swiftly apprehensive, without a clue to the identity of this tall youth who had confronted the tramp.

Pellman saw her and knew that she was the woman about whom the Greek had spoken. His eyes widened and he was visibly impressed by her beauty.

"Gosh, Jack, you're a picker."

"Look, Rita, this gent is Doc Pellman. He's the guy that put my conk together for me and done all this."

"Pleased to meet you," said Rita, chilly.

Pellman's hat was off. "Pleased to meet *you*, miss." He turned to the tramp. "Listen, Jack, I think I can get a compromise for you. They'll send you out into the county to some nice, quiet estate. . . ."

"Jack," said Rita, sharply. "Don't listen to him. It's a trap."

Doughface looked at her and felt the truth in what she said. "Look, Doc, geez, I'd like to help but I've bumped guys off. Don't forget that, Doc. I couldn't help it, but I did. You couldn't get these coppers to believe I didn't. Some of 'em seen me do it. If I turn myself in they'll burn me for sure."

"Now you leave that to me," said Pellman, knowing that he was winning. "I'll talk to the commissioner. . . ."

"No, you won't!" said Rita, growing tall and arrogant with anger. "You leave Jack alone. He can't help what he does."

"No, of course not," said Pellman. "But he can keep from doing it again."

"If I was only sure. . . ." puzzled Doughface.

Rita was thinking fast. She felt a debt of gratitude to the little man and, more, she knew that her lot would be misery if she was cast adrift now, beauty or no beauty. She had no illusions about this world, had Rita.

She glanced around her but nobody of importance or menace was in sight.

"Sure, Jack," Pellman was saying, "I'll see that you get a break. You just come with me. . . ."

And Doughface Jack was weakening. "Y'got a promise from the cops?" he begged.

"Well," hesitated Pellman, "not exactly, but I can be pretty certain. . . ."

She stopped listening to him, thinking rapidly. And then she did a most unexpected thing. She rushed forward, almost knocking Doughface down.

"LOOK OUT!" she screamed. "THEY'RE GOING TO SHOOT!"

And Doughface Jack's excited state of mind caused him to guess at a hundred troopers behind every pillar. A guard rushed forward, attracted only by the scream and Doughface multiplied him to a thousand.

With understanding, Rita dodged behind a nearby pillar almost before Doughface recovered. The tramp wanted to run, he started to run and Pellman, so close to success, did a foolhardy thing. He touched Jack's coat.

Doughface whipped around. Pellman staggered and began to sink down. The guard was coming faster and, seeing a man begin to fall, jerked out his gun and fired a wild shot at Doughface, high over his head.

Doughface glared in that direction, crouched to sprint away. The guard collapsed and skidded to a halt.

The milling crowd all faced toward the tramp and the two fallen men, and for an instant, Pennsylvania Station was hushed.

Another guard started forward from the press. He dropped. Behind him a patch of the crowd went down. The others stood for an instant and then an intelligent man in their midst knew and screamed, "IT'S HIM! IT'S THE MAN WITH THE EVIL EYE!"

Doughface glared after them. Few reached the door. The great marble blocks of the floor were covered with baggage and limp humans.

From the doors above the floor level a torrent of drab uniforms began to spew, flowing down. Doughface was breathing hard as he watched them. He thought he was trapped.

Sudden fury shook him. Why couldn't the fools let him be? Why did they have to keep leaping at him and hounding him and . . .

The OD flow turned into an avalanche. Weapons and hats and men cascaded down the steps, intermixed until there was no distinguishing anything.

Sudden fury shook him. Why couldn't the fools let him be?
Why did they have to keep leaping at him and
hounding him and . . .

The supply at the top ceased. A mountain was stacked up on the marble. An olive drab mountain marked here and there with bayonets.

Rita reached around the pillar and beckoned to Doughface. "Come on!"

They started for the train platform. But the noise above had already been heard and the news had spread. Not a switch-engine, not a porter was there to tip his cap and present his palm. Not an engineer or brakeman or conductor remained in sight or at his post.

Doughface halted on the platform.

"Geez," he almost wept, "we can't drive no engines no more'n we can drive a car. We got to get out of here, but . . ."

Rita was thinking fast again. She pulled at Doughface and raced up the steps again. Nothing had changed in the devastated waiting room. They picked their way, baggage in hand, across the sprawled and groaning people.

"Where ya goin'?" begged Doughface.

She did not answer but kept walking.

They reached the taxi lane but no drivers were there. Rita's flashing eye lighted upon a limousine which stood on the line, engine barely audible. She went swiftly toward it and looked into the front seat.

There, under the wheel, was a chauffeur. His eyes rolled white as he saw her and he tried to cower back.

"Get up," said Rita commandingly. "Who owns this car?"

"Miz Morgan Depeister," chattered the chauffeur. "Who . . . who you?"

"I want to help you," said Rita. "Sit up. Everything is all right now."

The man sat up. He saw Doughface but he didn't understand—not yet.

"Do you know who this is?"

"No'm," he replied, still too frightened to think.

"This," said Rita calmly, "is the man with the Evil Eye."

"Yassum. But I'se . . . HUH?" he choked suddenly. His eyes rolled back into his head and he seemed about to keel over. Rita jerked him upright by the scruff of his neck.

"You aren't dead—yet," she said coldly. "But you're going to be if you make one false move. Now listen. We are on our way to Washington, DC and you are going to drive us there."

"B-B-B-But Miz Morgan Depeister . . ."

"Did you hear me? This is the *man with the Evil Eye.*"

The chauffeur gulped. Sweat stood out on his forehead.

"Now," said Rita, "are you driving us to Washington or aren't you?"

"Yes," whispered the chauffeur limply.

"Doughface," said Rita, "would you help a lady into her limousine?"

Doughface Jack grinned and took her arm. They settled back in the seat, pushing the luggage out of their way.

"James . . ."

"My name is Sam," quavered the chauffeur.

"James," said Rita, "the White House, please."

Chapter Twelve

DOCTOR PELLMAN was not immediately cared for, as he appeared a shade more alive than the others who were being carried from Pennsylvania Station. All available crews of ambulance men in the city were hard at work striving to take care of the injured, dead and dying who were strewn throughout the station.

Doctor Pellman braced himself with his hands and through a fog of pain watched the harassed workers rushing in and out with stretchers and listened to the rising and falling chorus of sirens which rocked New York.

He must have been there an hour because an extra was already on the streets, being hawked in the station itself by now. Half of it was devoted to the chaos here and the other half to the hope that Doughface Jack and his mysterious "Witch Girl" were gone from New York for good. There was a rumor, the story said, that they had taken a limousine outside the station and had been seen again on the Jersey side of the Holland Tunnel. Destination was not definitely known.

It had happened that a news reporter with a candid camera had risked death in the station—and received it—by getting a shot of the pair and the edition promised that the next would carry that picture.

The picture had been published when they finally got to

Doctor Pellman. The second extra was being cried on the walk and as though from a great distance he heard, "Witch Girl, Queen of Beauties, aiding madman with Evil Eye. Beauty and the Beast join hands in devastation in Pennsylvania Station."

Pellman sank into a stupor through which the scream of the siren barely penetrated. He was not aware of being carried into a ward and laid, fully clothed because of the necessity for speed and the lack of helpers, on a white cot.

He did not know that this place would not long contain him and so he was very confused, two days later, to come more fully to life and discover himself in quite another place.

The room was a surgical ward, vaguely familiar. And it was not New York because the only sound was a robin's call. Pellman tried to raise himself and a gentle hand pushed him back. Bewildered, he saw that it was Miss Finch.

"Gladys," he whispered, weakly.

"Shhhh," she cautioned. "He's coming around, Doctor Thorpe."

Somebody else moved in the room and Pellman turned his head to his friend of long standing, Doctor Thorpe. The man was the greatest brain surgeon, according to repute, in the nation. His hands were those of an artist: sure and without a blemish to mar their smooth whiteness. His face was a very professional mask until he saw that Pellman had really come around. Then he relaxed a trifle.

"Well," said Thorpe, "I thought you were a goner, Jim Pellman."

"You would have been too," said Miss Finch, "if Doctor

Thorpe hadn't read your name in the casualty list and sent his ambulance all the way into the city for you."

"What did you do?" said Pellman, weakly.

"Series of transfusions, that's all. What else could I do? You, along with all the rest, had the worst case of anemia I ever hope to see, Jim. You'll take weeks to get well, even now."

Pellman raised up a trifle. "Is there any further news?"

"News? Well, no. That fellow seems to be gone from New York. At least nobody has seen him."

"I know where he is," said Pellman bleakly.

"Then you had better tell the cops," replied Thorpe.

"The police," sniffed Pellman. "And what would they do? Run out the riot squad and lose it to a man. Turn out the Army and lose that to a man. You saw what he did. Hundreds and hundreds of people . . . How many lived, Doc?"

Thorpe looked grave. "Don't excite yourself, Jim."

But Pellman was not to be put off. He raised himself into a sitting posture and when the room stopped madly spinning he focused his eyes on Thorpe. "You heard me."

"All right," fidgeted the great surgeon, "you asked for it. It takes a victim about three weeks to die. You were lucky. You weren't as badly hit as the rest and you had some care. But the others . . ." he shrugged. "Ten days to two weeks."

"We've got to do something, Doc," said Pellman. "We've got to do something! Don't you realize that all this is on my head? Can't you see it? I'm the man that gave him that! I'm the man that killed those people!"

"Please," said Miss Finch.

"'Please' be damned," said Pellman. "Don't you know what is going to happen? That girl is using Doughface Jack. Yes, she's using him. And she's taking him higher than he would ever have dreamed of going. He was a menace before. He's sudden death now. Doughface Jack is heading for Washington, DC."

Thorpe got it.

"You mean . . ." said Miss Finch.

"I mean he knows he isn't safe unless he's at the top. The girl has told him that. The papers are right. She's a witch. I don't know where . . ." He frowned. "Do you suppose . . . but no!"

"What?" said Thorpe.

"Maybe she's one of his victims. Maybe she's an old woman and the same thing happened to her that happened to me. Maybe . . ." He sat up even straighter and when Miss Finch strove to keep him from doing so he cast her aside with a motion he did not even know he made, so deep was his mental concentration. "Thorpe, I think I've got it!"

There was something in his tone which made Thorpe signal Miss Finch to stand back and not interfere. He poured out three fingers of whiskey into a beaker and handed it to Pellman who downed it.

"Yes?" said Thorpe.

Pellman took a deep breath. "Doc, you're the greatest brain surgeon in the world."

"There's some question about that since you fixed up that tramp," smiled Thorpe.

"To hell with that. You can do it all the time and I can

only do it some of the time. Listen, Doc, you've got to do something for me."

"Anything within reason," said Thorpe carefully. "You're taking this tramp thing too much to heart."

"Yeah," said Pellman. "Yeah," bitterly, "too much to heart. Only a few hundred have been affected so far. It's the nation tomorrow."

"The nation?"

"What do you think he went to Washington for? Play tiddlywinks with Grant's Memorial? That woman is clever."

"As for that woman, I can tell you something," said Thorpe. "When I was in medical school I saw her."

"What?"

"Yes, I saw her. She was an actress of some renown and an accident with hydrogen gas put out her eyes. I watched an operation which sought to restore that sight. That was thirty-eight years ago and I was eighteen. But I'll still remember her and I saw her again in that picture in the paper, bad as it was."

"That proves it!" said Pellman. "That proves it, don't you see? He made her young. He gave her back her sight. And she's got brains. She's had thirty-eight years of misery and she'll try to even up the score and with Doughface Jack at her side she can do it! 'Witch Girl' is right! But look, Thorpe, that isn't the point either. According to what I heard about a Greek he knocked out, Doughface Jack can undo his own work."

"Yes, somebody has been saying that in the papers too," said Thorpe.

91

"But he won't undo his own work because he thinks he'll be shot down on sight," said Pellman. "That leaves only one thing, Doc."

"What?" said Thorpe, unsuspecting.

"Thorpe, I know how I did that operation. Get me a stiff out of the morgue this afternoon and I'll perform it on that stiff while you watch. And then . . . Well," he said quietly, "then you perform that operation on me."

Miss Finch screamed and flung herself at the operating table.

Thorpe yelled, "NO! You damned fool! I might kill you with the smallest slip."

"That's my chance," said Pellman, an ecstatic light in his eyes. "That's my chance, Thorpe. I could heal those hundreds before they die. I could track Doughface Jack and meet him face to face without any fear. . . ."

"And maybe be burned to a crisp, both of you!" cried Thorpe.

"That's my chance. You've got to let me take it. You've got to! I did this thing. It's up to me to undo it. Get that stiff, Thorpe; we're wasting time."

Thorpe looked at him steadily for a long while and then, abruptly, about-faced and walked quickly to the door, determination in his every move. Outside Pellman heard him tell a nurse, "Miss Dawson, get a man from the morgue and have it sent in here."

Chapter Thirteen

THEY were parked on East Executive and they could see through the shady oaks in the park, past the statue of Rochambeau to the White House.

"I don' wanna," protested Doughface in a monotone. "I don't see no reason for doin' it."

Rita squared back in exasperation. "Jack, sometimes you can be very trying. Sometimes I think you're—well—dumb!"

He sat up belligerently but she smiled and patted his hand and he lost track of the conversation for the moment. He remembered shortly. "I still don' wanna. This put-together don't look right to me."

"Jack, do you want to spend the rest of your days in hiding?"

"Yeah, if nobody can find me."

"But that's impossible. If you got mad at somebody, the Army would be on the move again. You'd never be safe. You don't know this world like I do. You weren't blind for all the years I was. And blind, I saw much. People are rotten things, Jack. Rotten! Once everybody was my friend. Oh, yes they were. Everybody that was anybody knew me. Flowers and cards and invitations. And no dinner was complete unless I was there. And then it happened. Then I couldn't see any more. I was awful to look at. And what did they do?"

Her lip curled with bitterness as she thought about it. Her voice was like flowing acid.

"They forgot me. They left me to shift for myself. The men that I had befriended left me alone because I wasn't pretty any more. That was all they wanted from me. Beauty. And when it went, that was the end. You don't know what it means to be kicked into the gutter when the roughest fabric you had known was silk. You don't know what it means to try to fill a stomach used to scented wines with moldy bread crusts. Charity. I didn't want charity. I didn't want anything but the friendship which they had sworn they had for me. And everybody is like that, Jack. You know they are.

"Take this pal of yours, the doctor that made you that way. Did he stand up for you?"

"Well . . ." hesitated Jack. "No."

"Sure he didn't. He laid a trap and stopped you. He was trying to get you into the hands of the police. He was trying to stop you so that a man with a gun could shoot you before you saw him. You know that that's true. Pellman gave you the double cross. Those soldiers were waiting all the time. You couldn't trust Pellman and Pellman, from what you say, was the best friend you ever had. All right, add that up and what do you get?"

"I guess you're right," faltered Jack.

"You *guess* I'm right. You *know* I'm right. And I'll tell you something else. When I was at the top I had friends. Do you know who they were, those fools that threw me aside and forgot me when I had nobody?"

"No," said Doughface.

"No. No, nobody knows but me. The rest have all forgotten. They were kids, then, mewling around my dressing room door. They were down from Harvard and Yale and Princeton. And do you know where they are now?"

"No," said Doughface.

"On the bench of the Supreme Court of the United States. In the Senate and House. In the cabinet. Oh yes they are. Lots of them. And those that aren't own big factories and steamship lines. They're the pick of the country."

"Yeah, but . . ."

"And as long as they are up so high," said Rita, casually regarding the polish on her beautiful nails, "they can be used and, being used, can suffer. You and I, Jack, are going to show them a thing or two."

"But, geez," said Doughface, "I ain't got no idea about a gov'ment. I dunno nothin' about it."

"You don't have to know. You've got me. You don't even need to expose yourself. You've got a woman Friday."

"A huh?"

"You've got somebody to front for you and that somebody is me. Now come on, get out of the car."

She pushed him and he stumbled to the parking. The chauffeur looked anxiously for orders.

"Move one foot from here or say one word to anybody," said Rita, "and this man will track you to the ends of the earth to kill you."

"No'm," chattered the chauffeur. "I ain't gonna do nothin'. Honest. I just a poor . . ."

"Come on, Jack," said Rita, taking his arm.

He was very unwilling. He felt somehow that he was in the midst of a torrential current that was carrying him on and on despite any feeble effort he could make to breast it and gain shore. He was panicky when he thought that maybe these guys would shoot before he could do anything.

Rita read that thought.

"Now listen, Jack, this is going to be easy. All you have to do is look and they'll drop. They're after your neck. These men are the government. They're the ones responsible for all the police and soldiers in the country. If it weren't for these men you'll meet in a moment, you wouldn't be worrying the way you are. And they'd shoot you on sight, any of them. Don't give them a chance. I'll be right behind you so don't look back."

"Y'think I ought to do this? Y'think I *can* do it?"

"Do I think you can?" laughed Rita. "Why, I should say so. Nobody had better stand up to you, Doughface Jack. You're through being kicked around and starved and hunted. You're through with haystacks and boxcars forever. You're going to be the greatest man in the world and the only thing that's stopping you is a few men in the White House."

"Maybe I don't want to be the greatest man. . . ."

"You want me, don't you?" challenged Rita.

"Gosh," said Jack.

"Then you want to be the greatest man in the world. Remember that you are about to meet the men that have been hounding you. If they get away, you'll be killed. You must not let them get away."

Jack walked stiff-legged to keep his knees from buckling. But he was a little angry too to think that a few guys in a place like this could cause him all the trouble that he had been caused.

The gates were open as always and no one was on guard. The public was perfectly free to walk around this curving drive which led to the doors.

All was very peaceful. Cars hummed lazily along Pennsylvania Avenue behind them and a bored diplomat was getting out of his car in front.

Doughface was apprehensive about being recognized. His picture had been circulated in Washington because this very thing might happen. But he was fairly safe on that score. Rita had applied suntan powder, thus obliterating his most recognizable characteristic—his pasty white complexion.

Two Secret Service men were lounging in the doorway of the White House, on duty for this very purpose. They were young men, quick of eye and quicker on the draw.

Rita followed at a slow and casual pace. Doughface felt his knees knocking together.

The Secret Service men stood up straighter, as they did whenever they spotted a casual stroller approaching the driveway cover. Doughface walked along, trying to keep his teeth from chattering.

The Secret Service men saw Rita but still they were not certain. They glanced at each other as the visitors came even closer and then the shorter of the two reached casually into his coat pocket for the photographs.

"Jack!" said Rita tensely, "he's going to draw and shoot!"

Doughface thought so too. He started with the shock—and the thing was done.

The two Secret Service men stumbled back against the doorway. They sagged slowly. The shorter was attempting feebly to draw and shout but the lightning had stunned him.

Doughface wanted to run but Rita was treading on his heels. He went swiftly up the steps and across the fallen men.

The reception room had many people in it. And they had seen the Secret Service men fall and were coming forward wonderingly.

A guard saw Doughface and the collapse of the Secret Service men gave him the tipoff. He grabbed for his gun just as Doughface got inside.

"Back!" yelled the guard to the others. "IT'S HIM!"

In a wave of panic men dived for exits. But the offered weapon had done the thing once more. The guard collapsed, still fighting for a chance to aim the weapon. And then it was too late.

Three other guards went down like dominoes. The men and women in the room had taken too long to get out. They wouldn't now. They were lying on the floor in grotesquely twisted attitudes.

It was all silent, it was almost calm. It was horrible.

Doughface wanted to run again. But Rita held him by the shoulders. A door opened in reply to the shout and two more Secret Service men rushed out, to stop as though running against an invisible wall and drop.

Doughface heard a sound to his right and whipped about.

A guard was standing there with leveled gun. He fired a wild shot and then he went down.

Doughface dived for the inner chamber.

A secretary came halfway up from his desk and then fell face down across it. Three visitors leaped up and fell forward in limp heaps.

Another secretary came out of an inner office, papers in hand. He dropped and the sheets settled slowly over him.

"In there!" said Rita, shoving Doughface ahead toward a big door.

Doughface went forward.

The president had heard the first shout, the shot and then had seen his secretary drop. He knew what was coming. But he was no coward. He stood up, knuckles resting on his desktop, his face calm in its halo of gray hair.

Doughface came through the door and stopped.

"So you," said the president, "are the tramp. Has it occurred to you that you will undoubtedly hang for these murders?"

The statement could not have been more ill chosen. Doughface could not help his own reaction to that statement.

The president of the United States sagged into his chair, his face as gray as his hair. He held on hard to the arms of his chair, fighting to keep erect, fighting with more will power than he had ever known he had possessed.

"Don't kill him," said Rita swiftly to Doughface.

Doughface pulled Rita inside and then banged the doors shut. He turned again. He began to realize fully the awful thing he had done and he could see no salvation for him now.

The president of the United States sagged into his chair, his face as gray as his hair. He held on hard to the arms of his chair, fighting to keep erect, fighting with more will power than he had ever known he had possessed.

"Mr. President," said Rita, "you are not dead and you will not die if you do as I say."

Doughface thrust her aside, realizing fully what a spot he was in. "Geez, I dunno what I'm doin'! If I kill you they'll hang me sure!"

"Leave him alone," ordered Rita.

Doughface wouldn't listen to her. "I ain't done nothin' until now that I thought up myself. Geez, Mr. President, you ain't done nothin' to me. If you'll get me out of this jam . . ."

"Shut up," said Rita.

But the trick was done. The president had had enough to bring him back to himself again.

"Young woman," he began.

"Listen to me," Rita interrupted. "You're going to stay with us for safekeeping. They won't bomb this place as long as they know you're alive. They won't try to kill me because they will know that Jack is somewhere near at hand. Now he's going to bring your staff back to life and I'm going to start giving the orders around here."

"Why?" said the president. "What could you possibly do . . . ?"

"What could I do?" said Rita. "I can do plenty. There are a few men in high places, Mr. President, who are going to find out what I can do. If you want to live, shut up. A month ago Doughface Jack was nothing but a tramp. Today he's a bigger and more powerful national figure than you. Try and laugh that one off, Mr. President. Jack, get to work."

Chapter Fourteen

FOR five days Doctor Thorpe did very little besides sit at his desk and watch the reports stack on Doughface Jack. It was no longer necessary to clip the news stories but only to preserve the papers. A major depression was beginning on the wings of panic. No man knew what would happen within the next hour.

Rockford Sims of steel fame had died, suddenly and abruptly. Two cabinet members were being buried on this day, a senator on that.

And across the entire land there stalked the shadow of a beautiful woman, the Witch Girl, which name was no longer limited to the tabloids.

At first it had seemed impossible that anything drastic could happen other than a presidential assassination. No one had dreamed that the reins of government would actually be picked up and no man had been able to guess that there would be men more than willing to work for such a leader. Yet there were such men. They had been in minor offices where the work had been hard, the pay small and the bosses officious. And now they were only too glad to take allegiance and settle their own scores.

Democracy, in five mad days, had crumbled to a scrap of paper, and become what it had been in the beginning, merely an abstract idea. And now it was done. This was not monarchy, nor was it dictatorship. It was worse. The whims of a woman were deciding the policies of state and the personal animosity of a woman was passing the death sentence on every person who had ever offended her—and the offenders of a blind beggar are many.

Minority "isms" had fallen swiftly into line. Chaos had begun. A machine had arisen like a beast and would shortly be so powerful that nothing would ever be able to prevail against it. To the whims of the woman would be added the hates of lesser officers. Prejudice and jealousy and opinionation would rule the day. A system was rising and shortly that system would be too huge to be stopped.

The market had already crashed. Banks were closing every hour. Wild, insane rumors fled like tattered ghosts up and down the land. Men blew out their brains, bringing death before the death itself would come.

Thorpe watched his clock. He had watched that clock for five days and how slowly the second hand ran, how much more slowly moved the minute hand and the hour hand not at all.

For five days he had viewed and reviewed that operation, checking every step he had made, searching, searching, searching to be certain that there had been nothing forgotten, nothing left undone.

His buzzer rang and a nurse's voice said, "Doctor Thorpe. Doctor Pellman has just regained consciousness. He is asking for you."

Thorpe leaped up and, with shaggy locks streaming, raced down the corridor to the private room. He entered silently and stood, not daring to believe his eyes.

Pellman was sitting up with pillows at his back. He was smiling and, if it had not been for the bandages around his head, no one would have believed him ill.

"Come in," said Pellman.

"Jim!" said Thorpe hoarsely. "Then I didn't kill you after all."

"Kill me? I feel fine. How long have I been out?"

"Five days," said Thorpe, shakily. He approached Pellman's side. "But I don't understand. If you just became conscious, how is it that . . . ?"

"Same thing happened to Doughface," said Pellman cheerfully. "He couldn't heal himself all the way but he could come out of almost anything in jig time. What's been happening?"

"Jim, it's awful."

"You mean I was right? He went to Washington after all?"

"Yes," said Thorpe.

"The fools," growled Pellman. "I knew the police and Army would make that happen. They had to be bigger than either police or Army to keep alive. And what have they done?"

"It isn't so much what *they've* done," said Thorpe, "but there are others with plenty of petty scores to settle in blood. Plenty of others. And every agitator, every malcontent in the country, is swinging into line for them. It's the woman that's doing it. She had some grudges of her own and now all these others . . . Jim, I give the United States about two more days and then we'll make Russia look like a paradise. Pogroms, secret firing squads, espionage everywhere . . ."

"Then it's a case of stopping Doughface. What happened to him?"

"It isn't Doughface Jack. He's just the weapon of that woman. He wouldn't have the brains to do this," stated Thorpe. "Even I know that."

"Have they tried to shoot the girl?"

Thorpe nodded. "They posted a sniper on the top of the Department of the Interior and he used a telescopic sight. He hit her too. In the back. But the next morning she was out again and the sniper . . . he vanished. It wasn't Doughface that got him. They have the nucleus of an O Gay-Pay-Oo already. Men are going to them begging to be accepted. She ordered the release of all prisoners from the jails there and is going to release all other prisoners in the nation and, of course, they'll swing in. We're in for a reign of terror, Jim."

"I see," said Pellman slowly. "Do you think it can still be stopped?"

"As long as Doughface can kill men on sight he can't be caught. The president is held hostage and so the White House can't be bombarded. He got a message out requesting it anyway but the Army still won't act—what's left of the Army."

"What's left of it?"

"Certainly. The ranking officers are dead. They tried to hold conference and reach a settlement and the girl had them shot. There's nothing that can be done. Over twenty men have sacrificed their lives attempting to kill Doughface and his power seems to grow stronger. The president wouldn't believe there was any danger of this and now see what has happened!"

"Maybe it's not too late," said Pellman.

"It will be shortly," said Thorpe bitterly. "Business has stopped. Small officials have rocketed themselves to the top and everything in sight is being confiscated. Criminals will soon occupy the top positions in everything, and with their thirst for revenge against society . . ."

"How about the people that Doughface nailed before he left New York?" asked Pellman.

"Still about four hundred and fifty-odd alive."

Pellman threw the covers back.

"You can't get up!" said Thorpe, aghast. "After an operation like that you can't risk it! Why I took the top of your skull off."

"Doughface Jack's injury was complicated with trauma. Mine isn't. I'm all right, Thorpe. Get my clothes. Call all the hospitals and tell them to have those victims ready. We've got to make this fast."

"But wait," said Thorpe. "You're running a long chance! You may have a relapse!"

"Never mind that," said Pellman. "Get my clothes."

Miss Finch came in hurriedly, just having gotten the news. She saw Pellman starting to get out of bed.

"Jim!" she cried in alarm. "What are you doing?"

"I'm getting up," stated Pellman. "Don't stand there gaping at me. Get my clothes!"

"But," cried Thorpe, "we don't even know if it works with you."

107

"You don't, huh?" said Pellman with a sudden grin. "Go look in the mirror."

Thorpe glanced distractedly toward the one behind him and then started to say something. Suddenly he registered. He whirled around and bent over and studied his face.

"Why, why . . ." he stammered, "I . . . I look like . . . I look like a kid!"

"Get my clothes," said Pellman decisively.

Chapter Fifteen

DOUGHFACE JACK was sitting at the table in the White House dining room. Breakfast dishes were strewn before him, blanketed with the newspaper he was reading. Mechanically he dunked a doughnut in his coffee and just as expertly kept it from dribbling on his chin when he ate it.

Characteristically, he was reading the last pages first and at long last he turned and scanned the front page.

The scareheads hit him hard.

PELLMAN RECOVERS FROM OPERATION
MAN WHOSE SURGERY RESPONSIBLE
FOR TRAMP WELL

"Huh," said Doughface. "He got over it, the rat." He looked up and saw Rita standing by the window. "Hey, whatcha know about this? Doc Pellman didn't bump off after all."

She came to the back of his chair. "What else does it say, Jack?"

He read laboriously, "'Operated on by Doctor Thorpe, the famous brain surgeon, in an attempt to approximate the mito-genetic radiation used by Doughface Jack, Doctor Pellman was said to be doing nicely this afternoon. . . .'"

Rita's face was pale and her hand was like a vice on Jack's shoulder. "That means . . . that means that he'll try to get you!"

"Naw," said Doughface. "What could he do to me, huh? He's tryin' to heal up all them guys that I knocked down, that's all."

"What would happen if you met him?" said Rita.

"After the trick he tried to pull last time," threatened Jack, "I'm not taking any chances. There was a time I thought he was a right guy but when he tried to front for all them so'diers . . . Well, let me get a look at him and you'll see what'll happen."

"Maybe it won't do any good," said Rita.

"First time I ever saw *you* scared," said Doughface.

"I am—a little. Everything was going so well. I don't think we had better depend upon that trick of yours, Jack." She pulled the bell cord and went toward the door.

In a moment a thick-faced fellow came in. He bore the stamp of his past but even that harsh mark did not do that past justice. He had been everything from a dummy-chucker to a safe-cracker.

"Harry," said Rita, "there's a doctor in New York that's going to be able to do the same thing that Jack does."

"Huh?" said the ex-con.

"That's right," said Rita. "He's a tall fellow with wavy brown hair. You'll know him because he'll have the same expression around his eyes that Jack has."

Harry's stubby fingers touched at his left breast and felt the hard steel under his coat. "I get it."

"He's liable to come down here," said Rita. "Tell the boys

to keep a close watch and to shoot *anybody* answering that description that tries to approach the White House."

"Sure," said Harry. "I won't take no chances, sister."

He went out.

"Geez," said Doughface, "do you think that doc would come down here?"

"There's no telling," said Rita. "There's a chance that he's the only man in the world that you wouldn't be able to down. I wish I knew about such things."

"Aw, I'll down him, the dirty rat," said Doughface. "Layin' a trap for me that way. He'll mess around once too often. I'm goin' out and get Two-Finger to sit around and keep a special guard."

"You keep out of sight," said Rita. "You know what happened yesterday."

"Aw, they missed, didn't they? I'm sick of sittin' here twiddlin' my thumbs. I don't have nothin' to say or . . ."

She smiled sweetly upon him. "Don't get restless, Jack. As long as you're safe nobody dares touch me. And I've got this country in the palm of my hand. I ordered the release of all prisoners at Leavenworth this morning. Ricky the Mick is in for a stretch down there. He's worth having out."

"Will they release 'em?" said Jack.

"They better had. There's one thing they know we can do. We've still got plenty of important men in this city—men nobody wants to see killed."

"Y'think it's right to do that?" said Doughface.

"Anything is right that you can get away with," stated Rita.

"Yeah," said Doughface doubtfully. He looked back at the

paper. "Wonder if the doc is really goin' to come down here. Y'know, Rita, there's a chance he didn't trap me in New York."

"Nonsense," said Rita. "I've told you half a hundred times what he tried to do."

"Yeah, maybe you're right," said Doughface.

Chapter Sixteen

THORPE scanned the central waiting room at Union Station. He was extremely nervous as he had, from the first, opposed Pellman's trip to Washington, DC. And now that they were here, Thorpe expected death momentarily.

Pellman followed the redcap. There was a quiet certainty about Pellman. He knew that in a matter of hours he would either win or die. He had made his decision and on it he rested.

Thorpe paced beside him. "I tell you, Jim, this is nonsense. It was all right to cure up everybody in New York. That makes you a hero—hero enough. But . . ."

"It doesn't keep them from remembering that it was I that made Doughface Jack," said Pellman quietly.

"Sure, sure. But they'll forget that. They won't hold it against you. I admit that there's been a lot of talk in the press. . . ."

"Yes, lots of it," said Pellman. "They're damning me in every line. And why not? I was the cause of a half a thousand deaths. Maybe more. I'm the direct cause of this financial panic. I am the reason factories are closing and workers starving. If it weren't for me, none of this would have happened."

"Yes, but that's no reason for you to walk into a hornet's nest like this."

"I see that you are coming along," smiled Pellman.

"Well . . . yes . . . I . . ."

"But I'm not letting you come very far," said Pellman.

They were leaving the waiting room toward the cab line when a flurry of swagger coat attracted their attention. Pellman whirled to have Miss Finch fling herself into his arms.

"Jim, I won't let you do this!" she wailed. "When you vanished this morning I knew where you had gone and I flew ahead. You can't do this, Jim. It's suicide! He's got gangsters and everything! And you're all alone and you haven't even got a gun."

"I don't need a gun," said Pellman, gently pushing her away. "This is a deal between a girl named Rita and me and because of that I'll have to face Doughface. I don't know what may happen, but I do know that this is my fault. Nothing can stop me."

A cabbie was holding open the taxi door and Pellman started to enter.

Just in time, Thorpe saw the glint of sun on metal. He shouted "Look out!" and knocked Pellman back.

The gunman fired too late. Glass showered from the window. On the walk Pellman rolled swiftly over. The gunman was chopping down with a second shot. The gun blazed and the cab driver was hammered back against his fender. And then the gunman sagged, bending forward to fall without making an effort to break the drop.

"Get inside," snapped Pellman. "He must have people all over this town by now."

"That damned girl's emptied the jails," said Thorpe.

Pellman turned to the driver and stared for a few seconds. "Get in and drive, fellow."

The cabbie was holding his side and his face was twisted with pain. "I . . . I can't. I'm hit!"

"Sure, I know," said Pellman. "Get in and drive."

The cabbie pulled his hand away and looked at it. Yes, there was blood on it, but . . . but there wasn't anything more dangerous than a hole in his coat. There was no wound.

"What the hell?" he gaped.

"Drive," said Pellman.

They entered the cab and the driver began to weave through the traffic on the ramp.

"There might have been another one," said Thorpe. "They might know about this by now up at the White House."

Pellman looked steadily ahead.

"I'm going all the way with you," said Miss Finch.

"No you're not," contradicted Pellman. "As soon as we draw alongside another cab, I'm taking it. You can follow at a distance if you like."

"How," said Thorpe, "do you know Doughface won't be able to kill you?"

"I don't know that," said Pellman quietly.

Miss Finch was frightened. "Is it worth the risk?"

"Is the United States worth the life of one lousy doctor?" countered Pellman. "This is my show. Nobody ordered me to operate on that tramp. I operated and things happened. Nobody has ordered me to do this, but I'm doing it. It's the very least I can do."

They went around the circle at Massachusetts Avenue. The lights stopped them and Pellman, seeing an empty cab behind them, crawled out.

Miss Finch tried to grab his sleeve but he avoided her. "Jim," she cried.

He didn't look back. He opened the door of the other cab and got in.

"Where to?" said the broken-nosed driver.

"The White House," stated Pellman.

"Huh? Hell, buddy, you couldn't get me near that place for a million bucks. A thousand anyhow. What's the idea? Want to get yourself killed?"

"Maybe," said the doctor. "My name is Pellman."

"Pellman? *Doctor Pellman?*" said the cabbie with awe. "Gosh! Don't pull nothin' on me. Don't look at me. I'll drive you anyplace you say. Honest I will, only don't look!"

"All right," said Pellman, "I won't. But drive me around to the rear. I'll walk up out of the park to it."

The cabbie drove with a recklessness born of a desire to get rid of his passenger as soon as possible. He careened past the Treasury and around the curve at the back of the White House. He braked to a stop beside some masking shrubs and Pellman got out, reaching into his pocket for the fare. But the cabbie didn't wait. He was gone with roaring motor and out of sight in the blink of an eye.

Pellman turned toward the back of the White House. He was under no delusions about the danger he faced and in his mind stuck the words of Thorpe, "Might burn each other to a crisp."

The iron fence was high but Pellman had no difficulty in climbing it. He dropped to the lawn within, hidden from prying windows by a clump of evergreens.

And then began the work of edging up on the place, getting as close as possible before he was seen. And so swift were his rushes from cover to cover that he came within a hundred feet of the rear door before he saw a curtain twitch.

Window runners shrieked and a head appeared. The snout of a Tommy gun was thrust over the sill.

Pellman dropped just as the gun started chattering. Twigs and leaves sprayed upward from the tree above him. He raised himself an inch and stared.

Suddenly the gun began to shoot toward the zenith. And it kept on shooting as it arced. The last few shots sounded within the room.

Pellman leaped up and dashed for the door. A revolver banged to his right and a whistling bullet passed over his head. He flung himself into the cover of the doorway, glanced back and then threw the full weight of his shoulder against it. It crashed inward.

A revolver exploded almost in his face and a flash of pain raced up his arm. He did not see who it was as it was dark within this basement room. He did not have to see. When he started up the stairs he trod on an outflung hand which did not jerk back.

He reached another door at the top and slammed his weight against it. But he knew better than to go through. He jerked back and lead splintered the wood over his head.

He did not show himself. He, a man of science, knew a

few things Doughface Jack did not. Pellman stared through the partition, and though he saw nothing, there was a sudden silence in the White House kitchen.

He sprang into the room. Two men were heaped up before the stove. He heard a footfall in the hallway. He did not open that door immediately.

He waited and then he opened it.

A gentleman with a gun still clutched in his hand was face down on the floor.

Going at a run, Pellman raced toward the dining room. A gun crashed behind him and he flung himself forward like a slugger going for first base, glancing behind him as he slid. There was a thump and he did not need to inspect the source for the reason.

Directly before him towered Harry. The man gripped an automatic and his eyes were wild with determination to kill. But Pellman was still sliding when Harry got it. Harry stumbled back, arm going limp, a single shot pumped into the floor.

The doctor was up on the instant. He glanced about him. Somewhere at hand he would find Doughface and Rita. He had to find them before they could escape or before a lucky shot killed him.

He threw his weight against a double door. It gave with a splintering crash and Pellman braced himself from following through. Rita was just coming to her feet on the other side of a desk.

"Sit down," said Pellman. "I have no wish to kill you."

"JACK!" she screamed.

118

She grabbed for a revolver which lay before her and Pellman also snatched at it. The recognition of the danger in her had been enough.

Rita's stretching fingers suddenly tightened up into an agonized claw. Her face froze into white marble. She strove to stay erect but she could not.

She was dying and she knew it.

"Jack," she whispered.

And then, as though she were a puppet whose strings had suddenly been dropped, she sank into her chair.

A door was flung open and Pellman whirled to see Doughface. The tramp paused on the threshold. His hair was disheveled and his face grimy. He had looked for Pellman to come the other way and now . . .

"RITA!" he cried, rushing forward to grab at her shoulders. But even that touch told him that she was dead. He faced about, raging.

"Damn you!" screamed Doughface Jack. "You've killed her!"

"Jack," said Pellman, "you're coming with me."

"The hell I am!"

Jack drew himself up. There was a curl to his lips and hardness in his eyes. "You been askin' for this, Doc. I thought you was a good guy but I know now that you're just as rotten as the rest of 'em. I only wanted one thing in this world and that was this dame and now . . ."

He jutted out his jaw.

Pellman faced him squarely.

A grandfather clock out in the hall was tick-tocking with steady monotony.

Pellman felt as though he were being electrocuted but his face was without expression as he stood his ground.

The clock kept clipping the seconds and Doughface did not move. One of them had to break. One of them had to let down. One of them . . . And it was Doughface. He began to reel. He seized hold of the desktop to support himself. And then it came faster. His resistance vanished. He felt lightning frying in his head and awful nausea sweeping through his body.

He dropped, clawing out even as he fell to snatch a final hold. He knocked down Rita's arm and when he hit the floor, her hand was on his shoulder, touching him ever so slightly.

Pellman sank down into a chair and held his head in his hands.

Footsteps were coming from the hallway and then Thorpe was shouting, "We've found him! Here he is, Mr. President!"

A hearty voice was saying, "Thank God, you've come, Doctor Pellman."

"Jim," whispered Miss Finch.

Pellman looked at them sadly and then gazed upon Doughface Jack's outstretched legs which reached beyond the screen of the desk.

Pellman, at last, stood up. "Let's go," he said wearily.

The clock kept clipping the seconds and Doughface did not move.
One of them had to break. One of them
had to let down. One of them . . .

Story Preview

NOW that you've just ventured through one of the captivating tales in the Stories from the Golden Age collection by L. Ron Hubbard, turn the page and enjoy a preview of *If I Were You*. Join circus midget Little Tom Little, who learns from a set of ancient books on black magic how to switch bodies. When he jumps into the body of the lion trainer, he finds himself caught in the center ring surrounded by dozens of savage cats and quickly realizes that his craving for height just may have led him to a gruesome death.

If I Were You

HE had come as a mitt reader. Mrs. Johnson had not wanted to take him but, boss of the show though she was, she had not been able to refuse him. Hermann Schmidt, ringmaster and governor de facto, powerful figure though he was, had been unable to resist the eerie command of those eyes. And the man had become "The Professor" to the gypsy camp, and Yogi Matto to the chumps.

There had been uneasy speculation about him for weeks, for the breaks had been many—and all bad. But men were afraid of him and said nothing. As though finding flavor in his tidings, he had accurately forecast each and every disaster, even to this storm which had kept the crowds away tonight. And, weirdly, he had forecast, again with relish, his own death.

Some had said he was a Russian, but then a Hindu had come out of the crowd and the two had spoken in the Hindu's tongue. And when they had dubbed him as being from India, they found that he spoke Chinese and Turkish as well. A razorback had once seen the insides of his trunks and had pronounced their heaviness occasioned by fully a hundred books of ancient aspect, filled with mysterious signs and incantations.

That the Professor did possess some remarkable power

was apparent to all. For no matter how much anger might be vented against him for driving clients into hysteria with his evil forebodings of their future and thus hurting the show, no man had ever been able to approach those eyes.

No man, that is, but Little Tom Little.

Just how this was, even the Professor could not tell. But from the first, Little Tom Little, an ace at the heartless art of mimicry, had found humor in the Professor and had won laughter by mocking him. The matter had developed into nearly an open feud, but Little Tom Little, inwardly caring desperately what the world thought of him, but outwardly a swaggering satirist, had continued merrily.

The mockery always went well with the crowd, just as the Professor did not. Little Tom Little, in the sideshow, would get the crowd after the Professor was done and, very cunningly, would tell their fortunes in a doleful voice which made the tent billow from the resulting laughter. These crowds, sensing evil, had not liked to believe what the Professor had said.

And the gypsy camp had laughed with Little Tom Little, even though no man but he dared to affront the Professor.

The Professor had not forgotten his powerlessness to turn aside those quips. He had not forgotten that a man just thirty inches tall had held him up to ridicule for months. He had said nothing.

But he was dying now. And he was glad to die, secure as he was in a knowledge of the glories which awaited him elsewhere. In dying he would find himself at last. But he could not forget Little Tom Little. No! He would remember Little Tom Little with a legacy. He had already made out the paper.

Someone was coming up the aisle of the car, and then the doorknob rattled and Little Tom Little entered the stateroom. Water ran from his tiny poncho as he took it off.

The Professor moved a little on his pillow so that he could see his visitor, whose head was just above the height of the bunk.

Little Tom Little's handsome self, usually so gay, was now steeped in seriousness. He felt that he ought to feel highly sympathetic, and yet he could not understand exactly why, out of the whole crew, he had been sent for at this moment—for the physician outside had told him that the Professor could not last long. He was repelled, as always, by those filmed eyes, for Little Tom was not a brave man, for all his front. He waited for the Professor to speak.

"You are wondering," said the Professor, "why I have sent for you." His voice was very low and Little Tom had to put his ear close to the evil-smelling lips. "In your mind," said the Professor, "you are turning over the reasons for this. I must put you at ease, for I have always respected you."

Little Tom was startled.

"Yes," said the Professor, "I have seen much to admire in you. On the lot about me, men are afraid. They spread away from me when I approach. But you . . . you were brave,

Tom Little. You did not cower away. You had steel enough in you not only to meet me and speak to me, but you also had courage enough to risk my wrath—a thing which all other men feared."

Little Tom had not considered that his mockery required so much nerve.

"It was not courage," he protested, trying to say something decent to a dying man. "You just imagined—"

"No, I did not imagine. Men slink from me for a peculiar reason, Little Tom. They slink from me because I impel them. Yes, that is the truth. I force them away. I want nothing to do with men, for I loathe all mankind. I impelled them, Little Tom Little. Long before now you must have realized that I command strange and subtle arts beyond the understanding of these foolish and material slaves of their own desires."

Whatever Little Tom Little had expected to hear from a dying man, this certainly was far from it. In common with everyone, he had suspected these things, but he had been urged to derision instead of terror, not through understanding, but by nature.

"By such command," continued the Professor, "I am now able to leave this world for one far better, knowing exactly where I am going. But behind me I shall leave a little more than a corpse. I have a few things here—"

"Oh, you're not going to die!" said Little Tom Little.

"If I believed that, I should be very sad," replied the Professor. "But to return to why I brought you here; you must know that I was unable to make any impression upon you."

"Well . . . I never felt any."

"That is it," said the Professor. "I cannot touch you. And that means that you have it subconsciously in your power to handle and control all phases of the black arts."

"Me?"

"You. And I appreciate this. I respect you for it. I have a generous heart, Little Tom, for I am a learned man and can understand all things. Behind me I shall leave my books. They are ancient and rare, and most of them in mystic languages. But I have translated many of the passages into English. These volumes contain the black lore of the ancient peoples of the East. Only a few men have any notion whatever of the depths of such wisdom, of the power to be gained through its use. And you, Little Tom, are to be my heir. The paper here is witnessed. I give it to you."

Little Tom took the sheet and glanced wonderingly from it to the Professor.

"You did not believe I was truly your friend," said the Professor. "Now, what greater proof is there than this legacy so freely given? Does that prove my good regard, Little Tom?"

To find out more about *If I Were You* and how you can obtain your copy, go to www.goldenagestories.com.

Glossary

STORIES FROM THE GOLDEN AGE *reflect the words and expressions used in the 1930s and 1940s, adding unique flavor and authenticity to the tales. While a character's speech may often reflect regional origins, it also can convey attitudes common in the day. So that readers can better grasp such cultural and historical terms, uncommon words or expressions of the era, the following glossary has been provided.*

---

alum: a colorless crystalline compound used as an astringent, causing contraction. Used figuratively.

brakie: brakeman; railroad man in charge of the brakes.

bulls: cops; police officers.

bumptious: crudely or loudly assertive.

bunko: a swindle in which a person is cheated at gambling, persuaded to buy a nonexistent, unsalable, or worthless object, or otherwise victimized.

burg: city or town.

camion: a low flat four-wheeled truck, as for military supplies.

chumps: suckers; people who are gullible and easy to take advantage of.

cinders: incombustible residue of something burnt, especially small fragments left by burning coal. The cinders and ashes from a steam locomotive would often be cleaned out of the furnace and dropped onto the ground on and around the train track.

collar advertisement: collar and shirt advertisements by J. C. Leyendecker (1874–1951), an illustrator and entrepreneur who defined an era of fashion in the early twentieth century. He painted strong, athletic men and created long-running characters for the Arrow collar man ads (Arrow is a brand of shirt), as well as many others.

consumption: wasting disease; progressive wasting of the body; tuberculosis.

cordovan: burgundy in color.

de facto: exercising power or serving a function without being legally or officially established.

deuce, what the: what the devil; expressing surprise.

dick: a detective.

dummy-chucker: chucking the dummy; a type of beggar who gets money by pretending to have a seizure.

El: elevated railway.

fifty-leven: an expression used to describe a huge number.

Friday, woman: girl Friday; an efficient and faithful woman aide or employee. The phrase originates from "man Friday," as referred to in Daniel DaFoe's novel *Robinson Crusoe* for the character named "Friday," and later came to describe a male personal assistant or servant, especially one who is particularly competent or loyal.

ginks: fellows.

G-men: government men; agents of the Federal Bureau of Investigation.

goldbrickin': goldbricking; faking; posing; pretending to be something one is not.

governor: the head of the show.

hard lines: that's tough; something that one says in order to express sympathy for someone.

jake: satisfactory; okay; fine.

jig time, in: rapidly; in no time at all.

Ladies' Aid Societies: groups of women whose purposes included helping their local church and community. Often such groups conducted fundraising activities for their church and to aid impoverished members of the community.

Leavenworth: Fort Leavenworth; the site of a federal penitentiary in Kansas.

lucre: money, wealth or profit.

Mick: term for a person of Irish birth or descent.

mitt reader: palmist; palm reader.

Model T Ford: an automobile produced by Henry Ford's Ford Motor Company from 1908 through 1927. It is generally regarded as the first affordable automobile, the car that "put America on wheels."

nuts: 1. a source of joy and pleasure. 2. an exclamation of disgust or disappointment.

OD: (military) olive drab.

O Gay-Pay-Oo: a Soviet secret police agency originally called the GPU (pronounced Gay-Pay-Oo), which stood for "State Political Administration" and was later changed to OGPU when the Russian word for *consolidated* or *unified* was added to the name.

pince-nez: a pair of glasses held on the face by a spring that grips the nose.

Podunk: any small and insignificant or inaccessible town or village.

pogroms: organized, often officially encouraged massacres or persecutions of minority groups.

punk-water: the water that stands in rotten, decayed cavities of old trees. Called "spunk-water" by Mark Twain in *Huckleberry Finn*.

qui vive, **on the:** on the alert; vigilant.

razorback: circus day laborer; man who loads and unloads railroad cars in a circus.

right guy: good guy.

ringmaster: the circus Master of Ceremonies and main announcer. Originally, he stood in the center of the ring and paced the horses for the riding acts, keeping the horses running smoothly while performers did their tricks on the horses' backs.

Rochambeau: statue of the American Revolutionary War hero, General Comte de Rochambeau, in Lafayette Park, Washington, DC. As a French aristocrat, Rochambeau equipped a ship at his own expense and joined the Americans' fight for liberty and after the war he returned to France as a national hero. The statue was presented as a gift from France to the US in 1902 as a reaffirmation of Franco-American relations in the first years of the twentieth century.

rods: a pair of metal bars running parallel with the axle under a train car. "Riding the rods" was the true test of a hobo or tramp, who would swing under the moving train and climb along the rods to place a board across them and wire it in place. This created just enough space to lie on while the train sped over tracks only inches below. If the board was not wired in place, it could fall off when the train reached higher speeds; the fall under the moving train could kill whoever was riding it.

scareheads: headlines in exceptionally large type.

Scheherazade: the female narrator of *The Arabian Nights,* who during one thousand and one adventurous nights saved her life by entertaining her husband, the king, with stories.

set her cap for me: pursue someone romantically; to try to win the favor of a man with a view to marriage.

slouch hat: a wide-brimmed felt hat with a chinstrap.

snipes: cigarette butts.

stateroom: a private room or compartment on a train, ship, etc.

Tommy gun: Thompson submachine gun; a light portable automatic machine gun.

took to his heels: ran away.

uppers, on my: on one's uppers; poor; in reduced circumstances; first recorded in 1886, this term alludes to having worn out the soles of one's shoes so badly that only the top portions remain.

Waldorf: The Waldorf=Astoria; a famous hotel in New York City known for its high standards and as a social center for the city.

whippersnapper: an impertinent young person, usually a young man, who lacks proper respect for the older generation; a youngster with an excess of both ambition and impertinence.

L. Ron Hubbard
in the Golden Age
of Pulp Fiction

*In writing an adventure story
a writer has to know that he is adventuring
for a lot of people who cannot.
The writer has to take them here and there
about the globe and show them
excitement and love and realism.
As long as that writer is living the part of an
adventurer when he is hammering
the keys, he is succeeding with his story.*

*Adventuring is a state of mind.
If you adventure through life, you have a
good chance to be a success on paper.*

*Adventure doesn't mean globe-trotting,
exactly, and it doesn't mean great deeds.
Adventuring is like art.
You have to live it to make it real.*

—*L. RON HUBBARD*

L. Ron Hubbard
and American
Pulp Fiction

ORN March 13, 1911, L. Ron Hubbard lived a life at least as expansive as the stories with which he enthralled a hundred million readers through a fifty-year career.

Originally hailing from Tilden, Nebraska, he spent his formative years in a classically rugged Montana, replete with the cowpunchers, lawmen and desperadoes who would later people his Wild West adventures. And lest anyone imagine those adventures were drawn from vicarious experience, he was not only breaking broncs at a tender age, he was also among the few whites ever admitted into Blackfoot society as a bona fide blood brother. While if only to round out an otherwise rough and tumble youth, his mother was that rarity of her time—a thoroughly educated woman—who introduced her son to the classics of Occidental literature even before his seventh birthday.

But as any dedicated L. Ron Hubbard reader will attest, his world extended far beyond Montana. In point of fact, and as the son of a United States naval officer, by the age of eighteen he had traveled over a quarter of a million miles. Included therein were three Pacific crossings to a then still mysterious Asia, where he ran with the likes of Her British Majesty's agent-in-place

L. Ron Hubbard, left, at Congressional Airport, Washington, DC, 1931, with members of George Washington University flying club.

for North China, and the last in the line of Royal Magicians from the court of Kublai Khan. For the record, L. Ron Hubbard was also among the first Westerners to gain admittance to forbidden Tibetan monasteries below Manchuria, and his photographs of China's Great Wall long graced American geography texts.

Upon his return to the United States and a hasty completion of his interrupted high school education, the young Ron Hubbard entered George Washington University. There, as fans of his aerial adventures may have heard, he earned his wings as a pioneering barnstormer at the dawn of American aviation. He also earned a place in free-flight record books for the longest sustained flight above Chicago. Moreover, as a roving reporter for *Sportsman Pilot* (featuring his first professionally penned articles), he further helped inspire a generation of pilots who would take America to world airpower.

Immediately beyond his sophomore year, Ron embarked on the first of his famed ethnological expeditions, initially to then untrammeled Caribbean shores (descriptions of which would later fill a whole series of West Indies mystery-thrillers). That the Puerto Rican interior would also figure into the future of Ron Hubbard stories was likewise no accident. For in addition to cultural studies of the island, a 1932–33

LRH expedition is rightly remembered as conducting the first complete mineralogical survey of a Puerto Rico under United States jurisdiction.

There was many another adventure along this vein: As a lifetime member of the famed Explorers Club, L. Ron Hubbard charted North Pacific waters with the first shipboard radio direction finder, and so pioneered a long-range navigation system universally employed until the late twentieth century. While not to put too fine an edge on it, he also held a rare Master Mariner's license to pilot any vessel, of any tonnage in any ocean.

Yet lest we stray too far afield, there is an LRH note at this juncture in his saga, and it reads in part:

"I started out writing for the pulps, writing the best I knew, writing for every mag on the stands, slanting as well as I could."

To which one might add: His earliest submissions date from the summer of 1934, and included tales drawn from true-to-life Asian adventures, with characters roughly modeled on British/American intelligence operatives he had known in Shanghai. His early Westerns were similarly peppered with details drawn from personal experience. Although therein lay a first hard lesson from the often cruel world of the pulps. His first Westerns were soundly rejected as lacking the authenticity of a Max Brand yarn

Capt. L. Ron Hubbard in Ketchikan, Alaska, 1940, on his Alaskan Radio Experimental Expedition, the first of three voyages conducted under the Explorers Club flag.

(a particularly frustrating comment given L. Ron Hubbard's Westerns came straight from his Montana homeland, while Max Brand was a mediocre New York poet named Frederick Schiller Faust, who turned out implausible six-shooter tales from the terrace of an Italian villa).

Nevertheless, and needless to say, L. Ron Hubbard persevered and soon earned a reputation as among the most publishable names in pulp fiction, with a ninety percent placement rate of first-draft manuscripts. He was also among the most prolific, averaging between seventy and a hundred thousand words a month. Hence the rumors that L. Ron Hubbard had redesigned a typewriter for faster keyboard action and pounded out manuscripts on a continuous roll of butcher paper to save the precious seconds it took to insert a single sheet of paper into manual typewriters of the day.

That all L. Ron Hubbard stories did not run beneath said byline is yet another aspect of pulp fiction lore. That is, as publishers periodically rejected manuscripts from top-drawer authors if only to avoid paying top dollar, L. Ron Hubbard and company just as frequently replied with submissions under various pseudonyms. In Ron's case, the

A MAN OF MANY NAMES

Between 1934 and 1950, L. Ron Hubbard authored more than fifteen million words of fiction in more than two hundred classic publications. To supply his fans and editors with stories across an array of genres and pulp titles, he adopted fifteen pseudonyms in addition to his already renowned L. Ron Hubbard byline.

Winchester Remington Colt
Lt. Jonathan Daly
Capt. Charles Gordon
Capt. L. Ron Hubbard
Bernard Hubbel
Michael Keith
Rene Lafayette
Legionnaire 148
Legionnaire 14830
Ken Martin
Scott Morgan
Lt. Scott Morgan
Kurt von Rachen
Barry Randolph
Capt. Humbert Reynolds

list included: Rene Lafayette, Captain Charles Gordon, Lt. Scott Morgan and the notorious Kurt von Rachen—supposedly on the lam for a murder rap, while hammering out two-fisted prose in Argentina. The point: While L. Ron Hubbard as Ken Martin spun stories of Southeast Asian intrigue, LRH as Barry Randolph authored tales of

L. Ron Hubbard, circa 1930, at the outset of a literary career that would finally span half a century.

romance on the Western range—which, stretching between a dozen genres is how he came to stand among the two hundred elite authors providing close to a million tales through the glory days of American Pulp Fiction.

In evidence of exactly that, by 1936 L. Ron Hubbard was literally leading pulp fiction's elite as president of New York's American Fiction Guild. Members included a veritable pulp hall of fame: Lester "Doc Savage" Dent, Walter "The Shadow" Gibson, and the legendary Dashiell Hammett—to cite but a few.

Also in evidence of just where L. Ron Hubbard stood within his first two years on the American pulp circuit: By the spring of 1937, he was ensconced in Hollywood, adopting a Caribbean thriller for Columbia Pictures, remembered today as *The Secret of Treasure Island*. Comprising fifteen thirty-minute episodes, the L. Ron Hubbard screenplay led to the most profitable matinée serial in Hollywood history. In accord with Hollywood culture, he was thereafter continually called upon

The 1937 Secret of Treasure Island, *a fifteen-episode serial adapted for the screen by L. Ron Hubbard from his novel,* Murder at Pirate Castle.

to rewrite/doctor scripts—most famously for long-time friend and fellow adventurer Clark Gable.

In the interim—and herein lies another distinctive chapter of the L. Ron Hubbard story—he continually worked to open Pulp Kingdom gates to up-and-coming authors. Or, for that matter, anyone who wished to write. It was a fairly unconventional stance, as markets were already thin and competition razor sharp. But the fact remains, it was an L. Ron Hubbard hallmark that he vehemently lobbied on behalf of young authors—regularly supplying instructional articles to trade journals, guest-lecturing to short story classes at George Washington University and Harvard, and even founding his own creative writing competition. It was established in 1940, dubbed the Golden Pen, and guaranteed winners both New York representation and publication in *Argosy*.

But it was John W. Campbell Jr.'s *Astounding Science Fiction* that finally proved the most memorable LRH vehicle. While every fan of L. Ron Hubbard's galactic epics undoubtedly knows the story, it nonetheless bears repeating: By late 1938, the pulp publishing magnate of Street & Smith was determined to revamp *Astounding Science Fiction* for broader readership. In particular, senior editorial director F. Orlin Tremaine called for stories with a stronger *human element*. When acting editor John W. Campbell balked, preferring his spaceship-driven tales, Tremaine enlisted Hubbard. Hubbard, in turn, replied with the genre's first truly *character-driven* works, wherein heroes are pitted not against bug-eyed monsters but the mystery and majesty of deep space itself—and thus was launched the Golden Age of Science Fiction.

The names alone are enough to quicken the pulse of any science fiction aficionado, including LRH friend and protégé, Robert Heinlein, Isaac Asimov, A. E. van Vogt and Ray Bradbury. Moreover, when coupled with LRH stories of fantasy, we further come to what's rightly been described as the foundation of every modern tale of horror: L. Ron Hubbard's immortal *Fear*. It was rightly proclaimed by Stephen King as one of the very few works to genuinely warrant that overworked term "classic"—as in: *"This is a classic tale of creeping, surreal menace and horror. . . . This is one of the really, really good ones."*

L. Ron Hubbard, 1948, among fellow science fiction luminaries at the World Science Fiction Convention in Toronto.

To accommodate the greater body of L. Ron Hubbard fantasies, Street & Smith inaugurated *Unknown*—a classic pulp if there ever was one, and wherein readers were soon thrilling to the likes of *Typewriter in the Sky* and *Slaves of Sleep* of which Frederik Pohl would declare: *"There are bits and pieces from Ron's work that became part of the language in ways that very few other writers managed."*

And, indeed, at J. W. Campbell Jr.'s insistence, Ron was regularly drawing on themes from the Arabian Nights and so introducing readers to a world of genies, jinn, Aladdin and Sinbad—all of which, of course, continue to float through cultural mythology to this day.

At least as influential in terms of post-apocalypse stories was L. Ron Hubbard's 1940 *Final Blackout*. Generally acclaimed as the finest anti-war novel of the decade and among the ten best works of the genre ever authored—here, too, was a tale that would live on in ways few other writers imagined.

Portland, Oregon, 1943; L. Ron Hubbard, captain of the US Navy subchaser PC 815.

Hence, the later Robert Heinlein verdict: "Final Blackout *is as perfect a piece of science fiction as has ever been written.*"

Like many another who both lived and wrote American pulp adventure, the war proved a tragic end to Ron's sojourn in the pulps. He served with distinction in four theaters and was highly decorated for commanding corvettes in the North Pacific. He was also grievously wounded in combat, lost many a close friend and colleague and thus resolved to say farewell to pulp fiction and devote himself to what it had supported these many years—namely, his serious research.

But in no way was the LRH literary saga at an end, for as he wrote some thirty years later, in 1980:

"Recently there came a period when I had little to do. This was novel in a life so crammed with busy years, and I decided to amuse myself by writing a novel that was pure science fiction."

That work was *Battlefield Earth: A Saga of the Year 3000*. It was an immediate *New York Times* bestseller and, in fact, the first international science fiction blockbuster in decades. It was not, however, L. Ron Hubbard's magnum opus, as that distinction is generally reserved for his next and final work: The 1.2 million word *Mission Earth*.

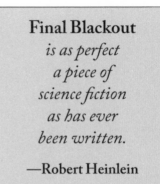

Final Blackout *is as perfect a piece of science fiction as has ever been written.*

—Robert Heinlein

How he managed those 1.2 million words in just over twelve months is yet another piece of the L. Ron Hubbard legend. But the fact remains, he did indeed author a ten-volume *dekalogy* that lives in publishing history for the fact that each and every volume of the series was also a *New York Times* bestseller.

Moreover, as subsequent generations discovered L. Ron Hubbard through republished works and novelizations of his screenplays, the mere fact of his name on a cover signaled an international bestseller. . . . Until, to date, sales of his works exceed hundreds of millions, and he otherwise remains among the most enduring and widely read authors in literary history. Although as a final word on the tales of L. Ron Hubbard, perhaps it's enough to simply reiterate what editors told readers in the glory days of American Pulp Fiction:

He writes the way he does, brothers, because he's been there, seen it and done it!

THE STORIES FROM THE GOLDEN AGE

Your ticket to adventure starts here with the Stories from
the Golden Age collection by master storyteller L. Ron Hubbard.
These gripping tales are set in a kaleidoscope of exotic locales and brim
with fascinating characters, including some of the
most vile villains, dangerous dames and brazen heroes
you'll ever get to meet.

The entire collection of over one hundred and fifty stories is being
released in a series of eighty books and audiobooks.
For an up-to-date listing of available titles,
go to www.goldenagestories.com.

AIR ADVENTURE

Arctic Wings	*Man-Killers of the Air*
The Battling Pilot	*On Blazing Wings*
Boomerang Bomber	*Red Death Over China*
The Crate Killer	*Sabotage in the Sky*
The Dive Bomber	*Sky Birds Dare!*
Forbidden Gold	*The Sky-Crasher*
Hurtling Wings	*Trouble on His Wings*
The Lieutenant Takes the Sky	*Wings Over Ethiopia*

FAR-FLUNG ADVENTURE

SEA ADVENTURE

TALES FROM THE ORIENT

MYSTERY

FANTASY

Borrowed Glory	*If I Were You*
The Crossroads	*The Last Drop*
Danger in the Dark	*The Room*
The Devil's Rescue	*The Tramp*
He Didn't Like Cats	

SCIENCE FICTION

The Automagic Horse	*A Matter of Matter*
Battle of Wizards	*The Obsolete Weapon*
Battling Bolto	*One Was Stubborn*
The Beast	*The Planet Makers*
Beyond All Weapons	*The Professor Was a Thief*
A Can of Vacuum	*The Slaver*
The Conroy Diary	*Space Can*
The Dangerous Dimension	*Strain*
Final Enemy	*Tough Old Man*
The Great Secret	*240,000 Miles Straight Up*
Greed	*When Shadows Fall*
The Invaders	

WESTERN